SPECIAL MESSAGE TO READERS

THE ULVERSCROFT FOUNDATION
(registered UK charity number 264873)
was established in 1972 to provide funds for
research, diagnosis and treatment of eye diseases.
Examples of major projects funded by
the Ulverscroft Foundation are:-

- The Children's Eye Unit at Moorfields Eye Hospital, London
- The Ulverscroft Children's Eye Unit at Great Ormond Street Hospital for Sick Children
- Funding research into eye diseases and treatment at the Department of Ophthalmology, University of Leicester
- The Ulverscroft Vision Research Group, Institute of Child Health
- Twin operating theatres at the Western Ophthalmic Hospital, London
- The Chair of Ophthalmology at the Royal Australian College of Ophthalmologists

You can help further the work of the Foundation
by making a donation or leaving a legacy.
Every contribution is gratefully received. If you
would like to help support the Foundation or
require further information, please contact:

THE ULVERSCROFT FOUNDATION
The Green, Bradgate Road, Anstey
Leicester LE7 7FU, England
Tel: (0116) 236 4325

website: www.foundation.ulverscroft.com

THE PASSENGER FROM CALAIS

After crossing from Dover, Colonel Basil Annesley finds himself to be the only passenger on the Engadine express from Calais to Lucerne. That is, the only passenger until a woman shows up at the last minute to book a compartment for her servant, an infant, and herself. Through the open window of his compartment, the colonel overhears their private conversation on the station platform, and is intrigued. The mysterious woman — a self-confessed thief, carrying something she refers to as 'our treasure' — fears she is being followed. Who is after her? What is her secret? And is she a criminal or a victim?

ARTHUR GRIFFITHS

THE PASSENGER FROM CALAIS

Complete and Unabridged

ULVERSCROFT
Leicester

First published in Great Britain in 1906

This Large Print Edition
published 2017

The moral right of the author has been asserted

*A catalogue record for this book is available
from the British Library.*

ISBN 978–1–4448–3478–9

Published by
F. A. Thorpe (Publishing)
Anstey, Leicestershire

Set by Words & Graphics Ltd.
Anstey, Leicestershire
Printed and bound in Great Britain by
T. J. International Ltd., Padstow, Cornwall

This book is printed on acid-free paper

FOREWORD

I desire to state that the initial fact upon which I have founded this story is within my own experience. I travelled from Calais to Basle by the Engadine Express in the latter end of July, 1902, when my wife and myself were the only passengers. The rest is pure fiction.

A.G.

1

Colonel Annesley's Story

The crossing from Dover to Calais had been rough; a drizzling rain fell all the time, and most of the passengers had remained below. Strange to say, they were few enough, as I saw on landing. It was a Sunday in late July, and there ought to have been a strong stream setting towards Central Europe. I hardly expected to find much room in the train; not that it mattered, for my place was booked through in the Lucerne sleeping-car of the Engadine express.

Room! When I reached the siding where this train de luxe was drawn up, I saw that I was not merely the first but the only passenger. Five sleeping-cars and a dining-car attached, with the full staff, attendants, chef, waiters — all lay there waiting for me, and me alone.

'Not very busy?' I said, with a laugh to the conductor.

'*Parbleu*,' replied the man, polyglot and cosmopolitan, like most of his class, but a Frenchman, or, more likely from his accent,

1

a Swiss. 'I never saw the like before.'

'I shall have a compartment to myself, then?'

'Monsieur may have the whole carriage if he wishes — the whole five carriages. It is but to arrange.' His eyes glistened at the prospect of something special in this obvious scarcity of coming tips.

'The train will run, I hope? I am anxious to get on.'

'But assuredly it will run. Even without monsieur it would run. The carriages are wanted at the other end for the return journey. Stay, what have we here?'

We stood talking together on the platform, and at some little distance from the railway station, the road to which was clear and open all the way, so that I could see a little party of four approaching us, and distinguish them. Two ladies, an official, probably one of the guards, and a porter laden with light luggage.

As they came up I discreetly withdrew to my own compartment, the window of which was open, so that I could hear and see all that passed.

'Can we have places for Lucerne?' It was asked in an eager, anxious, but very sweet voice, and in excellent French.

'Places?' echoed the conductor. 'Madame can have fifty.'

'What did I tell madame?' put in the official who had escorted her.

'I don't want fifty,' she replied, pettishly, crossly, 'only two. A separate compartment for myself and maid; the child can come in with us.'

Now for the first time I noticed that the maid was carrying a bundle in her arms, the nature of which was unmistakable. The way in which she swung it to and fro rhythmically was that of a nurse and child.

'If madame prefers, the maid and infant can be accommodated apart,' suggested the obliging conductor.

But this did not please her. 'No, no, no,' she answered with much asperity. 'I wish them to be with me. I have told you so already; did you not hear?'

'*Parfaitement*, as madame pleases. Only, as the train is not full — very much the reverse indeed — only one other passenger, a gentleman — no more — '

The news affected her strangely, and in two very different ways. At first a look of satisfaction came into her face, but it was quickly succeeded by one of nervous apprehension, amounting to positive fear. She turned to talk to her maid in English, while the conductor busied himself in preparing the tickets.

'What are we to do, Philpotts?' This was

said to the maid in English. 'What if it should be — '

'Oh, no, never! We can't turn back. You must face it out now. There is nothing to be afraid of, not in that way. I saw him, the gentleman, as we came up. He's quite a gentleman, a good-looking military-looking man, not at all the other sort — you know the sort I mean.'

Now while I accepted the compliment to myself, I was greatly mystified by the allusion to the 'other sort of man.'

'You think we can go on, that it's safe, even in this empty train? It would have been so different in a crowd. We should have passed unobserved among a lot of people.'

'But then there would have been a lot of people to observe us; some one, perhaps, who knew you, some one who might send word.'

'I wish I knew who this passenger is. It would make me much easier in my mind. It might be possible perhaps to get him on our side if he is to go with us, at least to get him to help to take care of our treasure until I can hand it over. What a burden it is! It's terribly on my mind. I wonder how I could have done it. The mere thought makes me shiver. To turn thief! Me, a common thief!'

'Stealing is common enough, and it don't matter greatly, so long as you're not found out. And you did it so cleverly too; with such a nerve. Not a soul could have equalled you at the business. You might have been at it all your life,' said the maid, with affectionate familiarity, that of a humble performer paying tribute to a great artist in crime.

She was a decent, respectable-looking body too, this confederate whom I concluded was masquerading as maid. The very opposite of the younger woman (about her more directly), a neatly dressed unassuming person, short and squat in figure, with a broad, plain, and, to the casual observer, honest face, slow in movement and of no doubt sluggish temperament, not likely to be moved or distressed by conscience, neither at the doing or the memory of evil deeds.

Now the conductor came up and civilly bowed them towards their carriage, mine, which they entered at the other end as I left it making for the restaurant, not a little interested in what I had heard.

Who and what could these two people be with whom I was so strangely and unexpectedly thrown? The one was a lady, I could hardly be mistaken in that; it was proved in many ways, voice, air, aspect, all spoke of birth and breeding, however much she might have fallen away from or forfeited her high station.

She might have taken to devious practices, or been forced into them; whatever the cause of her present decadence she could not have been always the thief she now confessed herself. I had it from her own lips, she had acknowledged it with some show of remorse. There must surely have been some excuse for her, some overmastering temptation, some extreme pressure exercised irresistibly through her emotions, her affections, her fears.

What! this fair creature a thief? This beautiful woman, so richly endowed by nature, so outwardly worthy of admiration, a despicable degraded character within? It was hard to credit it. As I still hesitated, puzzled and bewildered, still anxious to give her the benefit of the doubt, she came to the door of the buffet where I was now seated at lunch, and allowed me to survey her more curiously and more at leisure.

'A daughter of the gods, divinely tall and most divinely fair.'

The height and slimness of her graceful figure enhanced by the tight-fitting tailor-made ulster that fell straight from collar to heel; her head well poised, a little thrown back with chin in the air, and a proud defiant look in her undeniably handsome face. Fine eyes of darkest blue, a well-chiselled nose with delicate, sensitive nostrils, a small mouth with firm closely compressed lips, a wealth of glossy chestnut hair, gathered into a knot under her tweed travelling cap.

As she faced me, looking straight at me, she conveyed the impression of a determined unyielding character, a woman who would do much, dare much, who would go her own road if so resolved, undismayed and undeterred by any difficulties that might beset her.

Then, to my surprise, although I might have expected it, she came and seated herself at a table close to my elbow. She had told her companion that she wanted to know more about me, that she would like to enlist me in her service, questionable though it might be, and here she was evidently about to make the attempt. It was a little barefaced, but I admit that I was amused by it, and not at all unwilling to measure swords with her. She was presumably an adventuress, clever, designing, desirous of turning me round her finger, but she was also a pretty woman.

'I beg your pardon,' she began almost at once in English, when the waiter had brought her a plate of soup, and she was toying with the first spoonful, speaking in a low constrained, almost sullen voice, as though it cost her much to break through the convenances in thus addressing a stranger.

'You will think it strange of me,' she went

on, 'but I am rather awkwardly situated, in fact in a position of difficulty, even of danger, and I venture to appeal to you as a countryman, an English officer.'

'How do you know that?' I asked, quickly concluding that my light baggage had been subjected to scrutiny, and wondering what subterfuge she would adopt to explain it.

'It is easy to see that. Gentlemen of your cloth are as easily recognizable as if your names were printed on your back.'

'And as they are generally upon our travelling belongings.' I looked at her steadily with a light laugh, and a crimson flush came on her face. However hardened a character, she had preserved the faculty of blushing readily and deeply, the natural adjunct of a cream-like complexion.

'Let me introduce myself in full,' I said, pitying her obvious confusion; and I handed her my card, which she took with a shamefaced air, rather foreign to her general demeanour.

'Lieut.-Colonel Basil Annesley, Mars and Neptune Club,' she read aloud. 'What was your regiment?'

'The Princess Ulrica Rifles, but I left it on promotion. I am unattached for the moment, and waiting for reemployment.'

'Your own master then?'

'Practically, until I am called upon to serve.

I hope to get a staff appointment. Meanwhile I am loafing about Europe.'

'Do you go beyond Lucerne?'

'Across the St. Gothard certainly, and as far as Como, perhaps beyond. And you? Am I right in supposing we are to be fellow travellers by the Engadine express?' I went on by way of saying something. 'To Lucerne or further?'

2

'Probably.' The answer was given with great hesitation. 'If I go by this train at all, that is to say.'

'Have you any doubts?'

'Why, yes. To tell you the truth, I dread the journey. I have been doing so ever since — since I felt it must be made. Now I find it ever so much worse than I expected.'

'Why is that, if I may ask?'

'You see, I am travelling alone, practically alone that is to say, with only my maid.'

'And your child,' I added rather casually, with no second thought, and I was puzzled to understand why the chance phrase evoked another vivid blush.

'The child! Oh, yes, the child,' and I was struck that she did not say 'my' child, but laid rather a marked stress on the definite article.

'That of course increases your responsibility,' I hazarded, and she seized the suggestion.

'Quite so. You see how I am placed. The idea of going all that way in an empty train quite terrifies me.'

'I don't see why it should.'

'But just think. There will be no one in it,

no one but ourselves. We two lone women and you, single-handed. Suppose the five attendants and the others were to combine against us? They might rob and murder us.'

'Oh, come, come. You must not let foolish fears get the better of your common sense. Why should they want to make us their victims? I believe they are decent, respectable men, the employees of a great company, carefully selected. At any rate, I am not worth robbing, are you? Have you any special reason for fearing thieves? Ladies are perhaps a little too reckless in carrying their valuables about with them. Your jewel-case may be exceptionally well lined.'

'Oh, but it is not; quite the contrary,' she cried with almost hysterical alacrity. 'I have nothing to tempt them. And yet something dreadful might happen; I feel we are quite at their mercy.'

'I don't. I tell you frankly that I think you are grossly exaggerating the situation. But if you feel like that, why not wait? Wait over for another train, I mean?'

I am free to confess that, although my curiosity had been aroused, I would much rather have washed my hands of her, and left her and her belongings, especially the more compromising part, the mysterious treasure, behind at Calais.

'Is there another train soon?' she inquired nervously.

'Assuredly — by Boulogne. It connects with the train from Victoria at 2.20 and the boat from Folkestone. You need only run as far as Boulogne with this Engadine train, and wait there till it starts. I think about 6 p.m.'

'Will that not lose time?'

'Undoubtedly you will be two hours later at Basle, and you may lose the connection with Lucerne and the St. Gothard if you want to get on without delay. To Naples I think you said?'

'I did not say Naples. You said you were going to Naples,' she replied stiffly. 'I did not mention my ultimate destination.'

'Perhaps not. I have dreamt it. But I do not presume to inquire where you are going, and I myself am certainly not bound for Naples. But if I can be of no further use to you I will make my bow. It is time for me to get back to the train, and for my part I don't in the least want to lose the Engadine express.'

She got up too, and walked out of the buffet by my side.

'I shall go on, at any rate as far as Boulogne,' she volunteered, without my asking the question; and we got into our car together, she entering her compartment and I mine. I heard her door bang, but I kept mine still open.

I smoked many cigarettes pondering over the curious episode and my new acquaintance. How was I to class her? A young man would have sworn she was perfectly straight, that there could be no guile in this sweet-faced, gentle, well-mannered woman; and I, with my greater experience of life and the sex, was much tempted to do the same. It was against the grain to condemn her as all bad, a depredator, a woman with perverted moral sense who broke the law and did evil things.

But what else could I conclude from the words I had heard drop from her own lips, strengthened and confirmed as they were by the incriminating language of her companion?

'Bother the woman and her dark blue eyes. I wish I'd never come across her. A fine thing, truly, to fall in love with a thief. I hope to heaven she will really leave the train at Boulogne; we ought to be getting near there by now.'

I had travelled the road often enough to know it by heart, and I recognized our near approach only to realize that the train did not mean to stop. I turned over the leaves of Bradshaw and saw I had been mistaken; the train skirted Boulogne and never entered the station.

'Well, that settles it for the present, anyhow.

13

If she still wants to leave the train she must wait now until Amiens. That ought to suit her just as well.'

But it would not; at least, she lost no time in expressing her disappointment at not being able to alight at Boulogne.

We had hardly passed the place when her maid's (or companion's) square figure filled the open doorway of my compartment, and in her strong deep voice she addressed a brief summons to me brusquely and peremptorily:

'My lady wishes to speak to you.'

'And pray what does 'my lady' want with me?' I replied carelessly, using the expression as a title of rank.

'She is not 'my lady,' but 'my' lady, my mistress, and simply Mrs. Blair.' The correction and information were vouchsafed with cold self-possession. 'Are you coming?'

'I don't really see why I should,' I said, not too civilly. 'Why should I be at her beck and call? If she had been in any trouble, any serious trouble, such as she anticipated when talking to me at the buffet, and a prey to imaginary alarms since become real, I should have been ready to serve her or any woman in distress, but nothing of this could have happened in the short hour's run so far.'

'I thought you were a gentleman,' was the scornful rejoinder. 'A nice sort of gentleman, indeed, to sit there like a stock or a stone when a lady sends for you!'

'A lady!' There was enough sarcasm in my tone to bring a flush upon her impassive face, a fierce gleam of anger in her stolid eyes; and when I added, 'A fine sort of lady!' I thought she would have struck me. But she did no more than hiss an insolent gibe.

'You call yourself an officer, a colonel? I call you a bounder, a common cad.'

'Be off!' I was goaded into crying, angrily. 'Get away with you; I want to have nothing more to say to you or your mistress. I know what you are and what you have been doing, and I prefer to wash my hands of you both. You're not the kind of people I like to deal with or wish to know.'

She stared at me open-mouthed, her hands clenched, her eyes half out of her head. Her face had gone deadly white, and I thought she would have fallen there where she stood, a prey to impotent rage.

Now came a sudden change of scene. The lady, Mrs. Blair, as I had just heard her called, appeared behind, her taller figure towering above the maid's, her face in full view, vexed with varying acute emotions, rage, grief, and terror combined.

3

'What's all this?' she cried in great agitation. 'Wait, do not speak, Philpotts, leave him to me . . . Do you go back to our place this instant; we cannot be away together, you know that; *it* must not be left alone, one of us must be on guard over it. Hurry, hurry, I never feel that *it* is safe out of our sight.

'Now, sir,' Mrs. Blair turned on me fiercely, 'will you be so good as to explain how I find you quarrelling with my maid, permitting yourself to cast aspersions, to make imputations upon two unprotected women?'

'How much have you overheard?' I asked, feeling very small already. My self-reproach was aroused even before I quailed under the withering contempt of her tone.

'Enough to expect ample apology. How dare you, how dare you say such things? What you may imagine, what unworthy idea you may have formed, is beyond me to guess, but you can know nothing. You can have no real reason for condemning me.'

'Let me admit that, and leave the matter there,' I pleaded. I could not bring myself to tell her that she was self-condemned, that she

16

was the principal witness against herself. It would have been too cruel, ungenerous, to take an unfair advantage. Why should I constitute myself her judge?

She looked at me very keenly, her eyes piercing me through and through. I felt that she was penetrating my inmost thoughts and turning me inside out.

'I will not leave it at that. I insist upon your speaking plainly. I must know what is in your mind.'

'And if I refuse, distinctly, positively, categorically; if I deny your contention, and protest that I have nothing to tell you?'

'I shall not believe you. Come, please, let there be no more evasion. I must have it out. I shall stay here until you tell me what you think of me, and why.'

She seated herself by my side in the narrow velvet seat of the small compartment, so close that the folds of her tweed skirt (she had removed her ulster) touched and rubbed against me. I was invaded by the sweet savour of her gracious presence (she used some delightful scent, *violette ideale*, I believe), by putting forth my hand a few inches I might have taken hers in mine. She fixed her eyes on me with an intent unvarying gaze that under other conditions would have been intoxicating, but was now no more than disquieting and embarrassing.

As I was still tongue-tied, she returned to her point with resolute insistence.

'Come, Colonel Annesley, how long is this to go on? I want and will have an explanation. Why have you formed such a bad opinion of me?'

'How do you know I have done so?' I tried to fence and fight with her, but in vain.

'I cannot be mistaken. I myself heard you tell my maid that you wished to have nothing to say to us, that we were not your sort. Well! why is that? How do I differ from the rest of — your world, let us call it?'

'You do not, as far as I can see. At least you ought to hold your own anywhere, in any society, the very best.'

'And yet I'm not 'your sort'. Am I a humbug, an impostor, an adventuress, a puppet and play-actress? Or is it that I have forfeited my right, my rank of gentlewoman, my position in the world, your world?'

I was silent, moodily, obstinately silent. She had hit the blot, and could put but one interpretation upon it. I saw she guessed I knew something. Not how much, perhaps, but something to her discredit. She still was not satisfied; she would penetrate my reserve, overcome my reticence, have it out of me willy nilly, whether I would or no.

'You cannot surely refuse me? I have my reasons for desiring to know the very worst.'

'Why drive me to that?' I schooled myself to seem hard and uncompromising. I felt I was weakening under the subtle charm of her presence, and the pretty pleading of her violet eyes; but I was still resolute not to give way.

'If you will only tell me why you think such evil I may be able to justify myself, or at least explain away appearances that are against me.'

'You admit there are such appearances? Remember, I never said so.'

'Then on what do you condemn me? You do condemn me, I am certain of it,' she insisted, seeing my gesture of negation. 'Are you treating me fairly, chivalrously, as a gentleman and a man of honour should? How can you reconcile it to your conscience?'

'Some people talk very lightly of conscience, or use it when it is an empty meaningless word,' I said severely.

'You imply that I have no conscience, or that I should feel the qualms, the prickings of conscience?'

'After what you've done, yes,' I blurted out.

'What have I done? What do you know of it, or what led me to do it? How dare you judge me without knowing the facts, without a shadow of proof?' She sprang to her feet

19

and passed to the door, where she turned, as it were, at bay.

'I have the very best proof, from your own lips. I heard you and your maid talking together at Calais.'

'A listener, Colonel Annesley? Faugh!'

'It was forced on me. You stood under my window there.' I defended myself indignantly. 'I wish to heaven I had never heard. I did not want to know; your secrets are your own affair.'

'And my actions, I presume?' she put in with superb indifference.

'And their consequences, madam,' but the shot failed rather of effect. She merely smiled and shook her head recklessly, contemptuously. Was she so old a hand, so hardened in crime, that the fears of detection, arrest, reprisals, the law and its penalties had no effect upon her? Undoubtedly at Calais she was afraid; some misgiving, some haunting terror possessed her. Now, when standing before me fully confessed for what she was, and practically at my mercy, she could laugh with cool and unabashed levity and make little of the whole affair.

If I had hoped that I had done with her now, when the murder was out, I was very much mistaken. She had some further designs on me, I was sure. She wanted to make use of me, how or in what way I could not imagine; but I soon perceived that she was anxious to be friends. The woman was in the ascendant, and, as I thought, the eternal feminine ever agog to attract and subjugate the male, she would conquer my admiration even if she could not secure my esteem.

Suddenly, and quite without my invitation or encouragement, she reseated herself by my side.

'See, Colonel Annesley, let us come to an understanding.' She said it quite gaily and with no shadow of apprehension left in her, not a sign of shame or remorse in her voice. Her mood had entirely changed. She was _débonnaire_, frolicsome, overflowing with fun.

'What do you mean to do? Give me into custody? Call in the gendarmes at the next station? Have me taken red-handed with the — stolen property — the 'swag,' you know the word, perhaps, in my possession?'

'I am not a police officer; it's not my business,' I answered gruffly. I thought this flippancy very much misplaced.

'Or you might telegraph back to England, to London, to Scotland Yard: 'The woman Blair in the Engadine express. Wire along the line to authorities, French and Swiss, to look out for her and arrest preparatory to extradition.''

'I would much rather not continue this conversation, Mrs. Blair.'

'I am not 'Mrs. Blair,'' she cried, laughing merrily as at a tremendous joke. 'It is only one of my aliases. I am better known as Slippery Sue, and the Countess of Plantagenet, and the Sly American, and dashing Mrs. Mortimer, and — '

'Oh, please, please spare me. It does not matter, not a row of pins, what you are called. I would rather not have the whole list,' I interrupted her, but could not check her restless tongue.

'You shall hear, you must know all about me and my famous exploits. I was the heroine of that robbery at Buckingham Palace. I was at the State Ball, and made a fine harvest of jewels. I have swept a dozen country-houses clean; I have picked pockets and lifted old lace from the shop counters, and embezzled and forged — '

'And turned pirate, and held up trains, and robbed the Bank of England,' I added, falling into her humour and laughing as she rose to her full height; and again her mood changed, dominating me with imperious air, her voice icily cold in manner, grave and repellent.

'Why not? I am a thief; you believe me to be a common thief.'

4

I was too much taken aback to do better than stammer out helplessly, hopelessly, almost unintelligibly, a few words striving to remind her of her own admission. Nothing, indeed, could take the sting out of this, and yet it was all but impossible to accuse her, to blame her even for what she had done.

She read that in my eyes, in my abashed face, my hands held out deprecating her wrath, and her next words had a note of conciliation in them.

'There are degrees of wrong-doing, shades of guilt,' she said. 'Crimes, offences, misdeeds, call them as you please, are not absolutely unpardonable; in some respects they are excusable, if not justifiable. Do you believe that?'

'I should like to do so in your case,' I replied gently. 'You know I am still quite in the dark.'

'And you must remain so, for the present at any rate,' she said firmly and sharply. 'I can tell you nothing, I am not called upon to do it indeed. We are absolute strangers, I owe you no explanation, and I would give you none, even if you asked.'

'I have not asked and shall not ask anything.'

'Then you are willing to take it so, to put the best construction on what you have heard, to forget my words, to surrender your suspicions?'

'If you will tell me only this: that I may have confidence in you, that I may trust you, some day, to enlighten me and explain what seems so incomprehensible to-day.'

'I am sorely tempted to do so now,' she paused, lost for a time in deep and anxious thought; and then, after subjecting me to a long and intent scrutiny, she shook her head. 'No, it cannot be, not yet. You must earn the right to my confidence, you must prove to me that you will not misuse it. There are others concerned; I am not speaking for myself alone. You must have faith in me, believe in me or let it be.'

She had beaten me, conquered me. I was ready to be her slave with blind, unquestioning obedience.

'As you think best. I will abide by your decision. Tell me all or nothing. If the first I will help you, if the latter I will also help you as far as lies in my power.'

'Without conditions?' And when I nodded assent such a smile lit up her face that more than repaid me, and stifled the doubts and qualms that still oppressed me. But, bewitched by the sorcery of her bright eyes, I said bravely:

'I accept service — I am yours to command. Do with me what you please.'

'Will you give me your hand on it?' She held out hers, gloveless, white and warm, and it lay in mine just a second while I pressed it to my lips in token of fealty and submission.

'You shall be my knight and champion, and I say it seriously. I may call you to fight for me, at least to defend and protect me in my present undertaking. The way is by no means clear. I cannot foresee what may happen on this journey. There are risks, dangers before me. I may ask you to share them. Do you repent already?'

She had been watching me closely for any sign of wavering, but I showed none, whatever I might feel in my inmost heart.

'I shall not disappoint you,' was what I said, and, in a firm assured voice, added, 'You have resolved then to travel forward in this train?'

'I must, I have no choice. I dare not tarry by the way. But I no longer feel quite alone and unprotected. If trouble arises, I tell you candidly I shall try to throw it on you.'

'From what quarter do you anticipate it?' I asked innocently enough. 'You expect to be

25

pursued, I presume?'

She held up a warning finger.

'That is not in the compact. You are not to be inquisitive. Ask me no questions, please, but wait on events. For the present you must be satisfied so, and there is nothing more to be said.'

'I shall see you again, I trust,' I pleaded, as she rose to leave me.

'If you wish, by all means. Why should we not dine together in the dining-car by and by?' she proposed with charming frankness, in the lighter mood that sat so well upon her. 'The waiters will be there to play propriety, and no Mrs. Grundy within miles.'

'Or your maid might be chaperon at an adjoining table.'

'Philpotts? Impossible! She cannot leave — she must remain on duty; one of us must be in charge always. Who knows what might happen when our backs were turned? We might lose it — it might be abstracted. Horrible thought after all it has cost us.'

' 'It' has evidently an extraordinary value in your eyes. If only I might be allowed to — ' know more, I would have said, but she chose to put other words into my mouth.

'To join us in the watching? Take your turn of 'sentry go' — isn't that your military term? Become one of us, belong to a gang of thieves, liable like the rest of us to the law? Ah, that would be trying you too far. I see your face fall.'

'I am ready to do much to serve you. I would gladly help you, see you through any difficulty by the way, but I'm afraid I must draw the line at active partnership,' I answered a little lamely under her mocking eyes. Once more, as suddenly as before, she veered round.

'There is a limit, then, to your devotion?' She was coldly sarcastic now, and I realized painfully that I had receded in her favour. 'I must not expect unhesitating self-sacrifice? So be it; it is well to know how far I may go. I sincerely hope I may have no need of you at all. How thankful I am that I never let you into my secrets! Good afternoon,' and with a contemptuous whisk of her skirts and a laugh, she was gone.

'I'll have nothing more to say to her,' I cried in great heat, vexed and irritated beyond measure at her capricious temper. I should only be dragged into some pitfall, some snare, some dire unpleasantness. But what did I know of her real character? What of my first doubts and suspicions? She had by no means dispelled them. She had only bamboozled me by her insinuating ways, had drawn me on by her guileful cleverness to pity and promises to befriend her. I had accorded her an active sympathy which in my more sober moments I felt she did not, could not, deserve; if I were not careful she would yet involve me in some inextricable mess.

So for half an hour I abused her fiercely; I swore at myself hotly as an ass, a hopeless and unmitigated ass, ever ready to be betrayed and beguiled by woman's wiles, the too easy victim of the first pretty face I saw. The fit lasted for quite half an hour, and then came the reaction. I heard her rich deep voice singing in my ears, I felt the haunting glamour of her eyes, remembered her gracious presence, and my heart went out to her. I was so sorry for her: how could I cast her off? How could I withhold my countenance if she were in real distress? She was a woman — a weak, helpless woman; I could not desert and abandon her. However reprehensible her conduct might have been, she had a claim to my protection from ill-usage, and I knew in my heart that she might count upon a good deal more. I knew, of course, that I ought not to stand between her and the inevitable Nemesis that awaits upon misdeeds, but what if I helped her to avoid or escape it?

The opportunity was nearer at hand than I

thought. My kindly intentions, bred of my latest sentiments towards Mrs. Blair, were soon to be put to the test.

5

The train reached Amiens punctually at 5 p.m., and a stoppage of five minutes was announced. I got out to stretch my legs on the platform. No one took much notice of us; it must have been known that the train was empty, for there were no waiters from the buffet with *café au lait* or fruit, or *brioches* — no porters about, or other officials.

I had not expected to see any passengers come on board the train, a through express, made up of sleeping-cars and a supplementary charge on the tickets. But on running into the station (ours was the first carriage) I had noticed a man standing with a valise in his hand, and I saw him following the train down the platform when we stopped. He addressed himself to a little group of conductors who had already alighted, and were gossiping idly among themselves, having nothing else to do. One of them indicated our particular attendant, to whom he spoke, and who brought him directly to our carriage.

Evidently the newcomer was bound for Lucerne *via* Basle. Here was one more occupant of our neglected train, another companion and fellow traveller in our nearly empty sleeping-car. Curiosity and something more led me to examine this man closely; it was a strange, undefined, inexplicable sense of foreboding, of fateful forecast, that he and I were destined to be thrown together unpleasantly, to be much mixed up with one another, and to the comfort and satisfaction of neither.

Who and what was he? His position in life, his business, trade or calling were not to be easily fixed; a commercial man, an agent or 'traveller' on his own account, well-to-do and prosperous, was the notion borne out by his dress, his white waistcoat and coloured shirt of amazing pattern (a hint of his Italian origin), his rings and the showy diamond pin in his smart necktie.

I added to this, my first impression, by further observation, for which I soon had abundant opportunity. When the train moved on, he came and took his seat on the flap seat (or *strapontin*) just opposite my compart-ment. I could not tell why, until presently he made overtures of sociability and began a desultory talk across the corridor. My cabin or compartment, it will be remembered, was the last but one; the newcomer had been given the one behind mine, and here from his seat he commanded the whole length of the carriage forward, which included the compartment occupied by Mrs. Blair and her party.

I cannot say that I liked his looks or was greatly attracted by him. He was not prepossessing. Fair, with a flaccid unwholesome complexion, foxy haired, his beard cut to a point, small moustaches curled upward showing thin pale lips, and giving his mouth a disagreeable curve also upwards, a sort of set smile that was really a sardonic sneer, conveying distrust and disbelief in all around. His eyes were so deep set as to be almost lost in their recesses behind his sandy eyelashes, and he kept them screwed up close, with the intent watchful gaze of an animal about to make a spring. His whole aspect, his shifty, restless manner, his furtive looks, all were antipathetic and to his great advantage. I did not take to him at all, and plainly showed him that I had no desire for his talk or his company.

It was not easy to shake him off, however. He would take no offence; I was cold to positive rudeness, I snubbed him unmercifully; I did not answer his remarks or his questions, which were incessant and shamelessly inquisitorial. Nothing disconcerted him. I had all but shut the door of my compartment in his face, but it suddenly occurred to me that he was capable of wandering on, and when he found the ladies inflicting his greasy attentions upon them.

I felt that I had better submit to his unpalatable society than let him bore Mrs. Blair with his colossal impudence.

How right I was in this became at once apparent. He had taken out a cigar-case and pressed one upon me with such pertinacious, offensive familiarity that I could see no way out of it than by saying peremptorily:

'You cannot smoke here. There are ladies in that compartment yonder.'

'Ladies indeed! You surprise me,' but I saw a look on his face that convinced me he perfectly well knew they were there. 'Ladies, aha! How many, may I ask?'

'One at least, with her maid and a child,' I replied gruffly.

'And a child,' he repeated, as if by rote. 'Does monsieur, tell me quickly, I — I — beg — know them! Can he describe them to me?'

'I shall tell you nothing about them. What the mischief do you mean by asking me questions? Find out what you want for yourself.' I was hot and indignant with the brute.

'By George, you're right. I'll go and ask for leave to smoke. I shall find out then,' and he jumped up, the spring seat closing with a bang from under him.

The noise concealed the sound of the electric bell which I had pressed to summon the attendant, as I rushed out and caught the other man by the arm.

'You'll do nothing of the kind,' I cried with very vigorous emphasis, backed by all my strength. 'I'll shake you to a jelly if you dare to move another inch.'

'Here, I say, drop it. Who the deuce are you? None of your bally nonsense. Hands off, or I'll make you.'

But he was too soft and flabby to avail much, and I dragged him back helplessly with tightened grip, only too delighted to try conclusions with him.

At this moment the conductor appeared upon the scene, and began to expostulate loudly.

'Here, I say, what's all this? It can't be allowed. No fighting and quarrelling are permitted.'

'Well, then, people must behave themselves,' I retorted. 'Don't let this chap annoy your passengers.'

'I have done nothing to annoy them,' stammered the other. 'You shall answer for this. I've done no harm.'

'I'll see you don't. Get in there and stay there;' and with that I forced him, almost flung him, into his compartment, where he fell panting upon the velvet sofa.

'You'd better keep an eye on him,' I said to the conductor, who was inclined to be disagreeable, and was barely pacified by a couple of five-franc pieces. 'Fellows of this sort are apt to be a nuisance, and we must take care of the ladies.'

As I said this I saw Mrs. Blair's face peering out beyond her door a little nervously, but she ventured to come right out and along the passage towards me.

'What has happened? I heard some noise, high words, a scuffle.'

'Some ruffian who got in at Amiens, and who has had to be taught manners. I told him not to smoke here, and he wanted to intrude himself upon you, which I prevented, a little forcibly.'

'Where is he? In here?' and she followed the indication of my thumb as I jerked it back, and looked over my shoulder into the compartment.

'Ah!' The ejaculation was involuntary, and one of acute painful surprise, the gesture that accompanied it spontaneous and full of terror.

'That man! that man!' she gasped. 'He must not see me; let me go, let me go!'

But her strength failed her, and but for my

supporting arm she would have fallen to the ground. Half-fainting, I led her back to her own compartment, where her maid received her tenderly and with comforting words. There was clearly a strong bond of affection between these two, possibly companions and confederates in wrong-doing; the delicate and refined woman, tormented by the inner qualms of outraged conscience, relied and leant upon the stronger and more resolute nature.

'What's come to you, ma'am? There, there, don't give way,' said the maid, softly coaxing her and stroking her hands.

'Oh, Philpotts, fancy! He is there! Falfani, the — the — you know — '

Of course I saw it all now. Stupid ass! I might have guessed it all along. I had puzzled my brains vainly trying to place him, to fix his quality and condition in life, neglecting the one simple obvious solution to which so many plain indications pointed. The man, of course, was a detective, an officer or private agent, and his dirty business — you see, I was already shaken in my honesty, and now with increasing demoralization under seductive influences I was already inclined to cross over to the other side of the frontier of crime — his dirty business was the persecution of my sweet friend.

'What are we to do now?' asked Mrs. Blair, her nervous trepidation increasing. 'I begin to think we shall fail, we cannot carry it through, we shall lose our treasure. It will be taken from us.'

'You cannot, you must not, shall not turn back now,' said the maid with great determination. 'We must devise something, some way, of outwitting this Falfani. We did it before, we must do it again. After all he has no power over us; we are in France and shall be in Switzerland by daylight.'

'We ought to go on, you think? Wouldn't it be better to slip out of the train at the first station and run away?'

'He would do the same. He does not intend to let us out of his sight. And how much the better should we be? It would be far worse; we should be much more at his mercy if we left the train. The journey would still have to be made; we must get to the end, the very end, or we'd better not have started.'

'He will know then, if he sticks to us. We cannot hide it from him, nor where we have taken it; we shall never be able to keep it, they will come and claim it and recover it;' and she cried hysterically: 'I cannot see my way; it's all dark, black as night. I wish — I wish — '

'That you had never done it?' quickly asked the maid; and I noticed a slight sarcasm in

37

her tone that was not without its effect in bracing up and strengthening her companion's shattered nerves.

'No, no, no; I do not regret it, and I never shall. I did it deliberately, counting the cost fully, and it shall be paid, however heavy it may be. It is not regret that tortures me, but the fear of failure when so near success.'

'We will succeed yet. Do not be cast down, my sweet dear.' The maid patted her on the cheek with great affection. 'We shall find a way. This gentleman, the colonel here, will help us, perhaps.'

'Will you?' Who could resist her pleading voice and shining eyes? If I had had any scruples left I would have thrown them to the winds.

'Whatever lies in my power to do shall be done without stint or hesitation,' I said solemnly, careless of all consequences, content to hold her hand and earn her heartfelt thanks. What though I were pawning my honour?

6

The Statement of Domenico Falfani, confidential agent, made to his employers, Messrs. Becke and Co., of the Private Inquiry Offices, 279 St. Martin's Lane, W.C.

I propose, gentlemen, to set down here at length the story of my mission, and the events which befell me from the time I first received my instructions. You desired me to pursue and call to strict account a certain lady of title, who had fallen away from her high estate and committed an act of rank felony. The circumstances which led up to her disappearance and the partners of her flight are already well known to you.

The only indication given me, as you are aware, was that I might take it for granted that she would go abroad and probably by the most direct route to the South, to Switzerland and across the Alps into Italy. My orders having only reached me in the early morning, the theft having presumably been committed during the night previous to Sunday, September 21, I was unable to ascertain through the tourist agencies whether any and what tickets had been booked in the directions indicated.

My most urgent duty then was to watch the outgoing Continental trains, the first of which left Charing Cross for Dover and Calais at 9 a.m. I closely watched it therefore, and its passengers, and travelled with it to Cannon Street, where I continued my search, but without result. I was greatly helped in my quest by the not unusual fact noticeable on Sundays, that travellers abroad are few in number.

I had no difficulty in satisfying myself that the lady and her party were not in this train, and I returned at once to Charing Cross in time for the second Continental train, the 10 a.m.

I had resolved to book myself by that as far as Amiens, for I knew that, once there, I should have reached a central point or junction, a sort of throat through which every train moving southward to Paris or Switzerland must pass.

There remained, of course, the route via Dover by Ostend and through Brussels; but I had been informed by you that Ludovic Tiler, my colleague and coworker, was to undertake the inquiry on that line.

It is part of my business to be thoroughly familiar with the Continental Bradshaw, and I soon ticked off the different trains that interested me.

There was first the 11 a.m. from Victoria by Dover and Calais, where it connected with the Paris express and the sleeping-car Engadine express, both of which run through Amiens, where, however, the latter branches off to Basle and beyond, with special cars for Lucerne, Zurich and Coire.

Then came the 2.20 p.m. from Charing Cross to Folkestone, and so to Boulogne, Amiens and the rest, travelling the same road as the Engadine express. This was the last of the day service, as it gave most time, allowing people to start at the very latest moment, and I felt it quite probable that my lady would prefer to take it.

I reached Amiens a little before 5 p.m., and I had a wait of half an hour for the first express from Calais. I was greatly disappointed when at last it appeared issuing from the tunnel, and passed me where I stood at the commencement of the platform, taking stock of each carriage as it passed. The train seemed to be quite empty; there were no passengers, so the officials, the conductors, informed me when I talked to them, sad and unhappy at the certain loss of tips. Only one of them had any luck, Jules l'Echelle, of the Lucerne sleeping-car, who had one or two people on board.

I questioned him not very hopefully, but

was agreeably surprised when he told me that his clients consisted of two ladies with a child, and one gentleman. English? Yes, all English. The lady, quite a lady, a *grande dame belle personne*, tall, fine figure, well dressed; her companion no doubt her servant; the child, well, an ordinary child, an infant in arms. What would you?

I had them, I felt sure. There could be no mistaking this description. I held them in the hollow of my hand. Here they were in this car, and it would be all my own fault if they escaped me. It would be necessary only to verify my conclusions, to identify the lady according to the description and photograph given me. For the rest I knew what to do.

But now a quite unexpected difficulty turned up.

As I have said, there was one other passenger, a gentleman, in the car, and I felt it would be prudent to make his acquaintance. No doubt I could tell at the first glance whether or not he was an ordinary traveller, or whether he was a friend and accomplice of the lady under observation.

I regret to say that he met me in a very hostile spirit. I was at great pains to be affable, to treat him with all the courtly consideration I have at command, and I flatter myself that in the matter of tact and good-breeding I do not yield to princes of the blood royal. But my civility was quite thrown away. The man was an absolute brute, abrupt, overbearing, rude. Nothing would conciliate him. I offered him a cigar (a Borneo of the best brand, at 10s. the hundred), and he not only refused it, but positively forbade me to smoke. There were ladies in the carriage, he said (this was the first reference made to them), and, when declining to be ordered about, I proposed to refer the question to themselves, he threw himself violently upon me and assaulted me brutally.

Fortunately the attendant came to my rescue or I should have been seriously injured. He lifted me into my compartment very kindly, and acted like an old friend, as indeed he was, for I remembered him as the Jules l'Echelle with whom I served some time back as an assistant at the Baths of Bormio.

It was, of course, clear to my mind that my assailant was associated in some way with the lady, and probably a confederate. I saw that I must know more about him, with the least possible delay, and as soon as Jules had left me, promising to return later and talk of old times, and the changes that had come over us since then, I ventured to look out and get a glimpse of the other man, I will not call him gentleman after his conduct.

He was nowhere in sight, but I could hear his voice, several voices, talking together at the far end. No doubt he had joined his friends in their compartment, and the moment seemed opportune to visit his. It was next to mine, and the door stood invitingly open. A few minutes, seconds even, would be enough to tell me something of his identity, perhaps all I wanted to.

At least he made no pretence at mystery; his light baggage lay about, a dressing bag, a roll of rugs, a couple of sticks and an umbrella strapped together, all very neat and precise and respectable, and all alike furnished with a parchment tag or label bearing in plain language all that I wanted to know.

His name was printed 'Lieut.-Col. Basil Annesley,' and his club, the Mars and Neptune, that famous military house in Piccadilly. Underneath, on all, his destination was written, 'Hotel Bellevue, Bellagio, Como.' There could never be the least difficulty in finding this person if I wanted him, as I thought likely. He was a blustering, swash-buckling army officer, who could always be brought to account if he misconducted himself, or mixed himself up in shady transactions.

In my great contentment at the discovery I had been wanting in caution, and I lingered too long on forbidden ground.

'You infernal scoundrel,' cried some one from the door, and once more I felt an angry hand on my shoulder. 'How come you here? Explain yourself.'

'It's all a mistake,' I began, trying to make the best of it, struggling to get free. But he still held me in a grip of iron, and it was not until my friend Jules appeared that I got out of the enemy's clutches.

'Here, I say!' shouted Jules vaguely. 'This won't do, you know. I shall have to lodge a complaint against you for brawling.'

'Complaint, by George!' he replied, shaking his fist at me. 'The boot is on the other leg, I take it. How is it that I find this chap in my compartment? Foraging about, I believe.'

'Indeed no, Colonel Annesley,' I protested, forgetting myself; and he caught at it directly.

'Oho, so you know my name! That proves what I say. You've been messing about and overhauling my things. I won't stand it. The man's a thief. He will have to be locked up.'

'I'm not the only thief in the car, then,' I cried, for I was now mad with him and his threats.

'I don't know what you're driving at, or whom you think to accuse; but I tell you this, my friend, that I shall call in the police at the next station and hand you over.'

I looked at the conductor Jules, appealing for protection. I saw at once that it would be terrible for me to have any trouble with the police. They could do me no harm, but I might be delayed, obliged to leave the train, and I should lose sight of the lady, possibly fail altogether.

Jules responded at once. 'Come, come,' he said. 'You're talking big. You might own the whole train. Who might you be?'

'None of your confounded impudence,' shouted the Colonel, as he pointed to one of the luggage labels. 'That's who I am. It's good enough to get you discharged before you're a much older man. And now I call upon you to do your duty. I have caught this man under suspicious circumstances in the very act of rifling my effects. I insist upon his being taken into custody.'

'There isn't enough for that,' Jules answered, still my friend, but weakening a little before this masterly army officer, and I felt that I must speak for myself.

'And if you stop me I will have the law of you for false imprisonment, and bring heavy damages. You will be doing me a great injury in my business.'

'Precisely what I should like to do, my fine fellow. I can guess what your business is. Nothing reputable, I feel sure.'

'I'm not ashamed of it, and I have powerful friends behind me. I am acting for — '

'Yes?' he asked me mockingly, for I had checked my tongue, fearing to say too much.

'It is my affair. Enough that you will feel the weight of their hands if you interfere with me in carrying out their instructions.'

'Well, anyhow, tell me who you are. I've a right to know that in exchange. You chose to help yourself to my name; now I insist upon knowing yours.'

I told him, not very readily, as may be supposed.

'Domenico Falfani? Is that your own or a 'purser's' name? Come, you know what I mean. It's part of your stock in trade to understand all languages, including slang. Is that the name he has given you?' — this to the conductor. 'Show me your way-bill, your *feuille de route.*'

Jules at a nod from me produced it, and no doubt understood my reason when in my turn I claimed to see it.

'I have a clear right,' I insisted, overruling all objections raised by the Colonel; and taking it into my hands I read the names aloud, 'Colonel Annesley, Mrs. Blair, maid and child.' I pronounced the name with great contempt.

'You talk of purser's names,' I said

sneeringly. 'What do you think of this? Blair, indeed! No more the woman's name than Smith or Jones, or what you please.'

'Speak more respectfully of a lady,' cried the Colonel, catching me tightly by the arm.

'Lady? Oho! Don't, Colonel, drop it. At any rate, she is not Mrs. Blair; you may take that from me,' I said as impressively as a judge on the bench. 'And what's more, Colonel, I wouldn't press charges you can't substantiate against me, or I may hit back with another not so easy to meet. Try to stop me at the next station, and I'll stop your pal — ah, don't' — he had a cruelly strong hand — 'your Mrs. Blair, and she'll find herself in a particularly tight place.'

'We'll see about that,' said the Colonel, who kept a stiff face, but was, I think, rather crestfallen. 'I shall act as I think best. Anyhow, get out of this, both of you. This is my private berth, and you are trespassing.'

7

Whatever may have been the Colonel's intentions when he caught me in his compartment, something, and I think my last words, led him to modify them. He felt, probably, that if he attacked me I might retaliate unpleasantly. I ought to be able to hold my own with him, although in truth I was not over happy at the course events had taken, and I could not compliment myself on my good management.

I had not been overprudent; I had pressed my attentions on him rather abruptly, although I had the excuse that I usually found them well received, thanks to my affable address; again I had behaved most incautiously in penetrating his identity.

And, worse than all, I had still no certainty. I could only surmise that the lady was the one I was in search of, for I had not as yet clapped eyes on her, and I had been to some extent driven to show my hand before I had made my ground good. So the first thing I did on regaining my own compartment was to ring for Jules, the conductor, and put before him the photograph with which I was provided, and ask him if he recognized it.

'But perfectly. It is the lady yonder,' he said promptly. 'Is it your own, or did you find it or annex it from next door? Ah, your own; and what have you to do with her?'

'I may tell you some day, Jules. For the present you must know that I am after her; I have to watch her, stick to her like her shadow until it is time to act.'

'An adventuress, eh?'

'She is in possession of what does not belong to her; something she abstracted from from — Never mind where, and it must be recovered from her here, or after she leaves the car.'

'Afterwards, please. We can't have any scandal on board here.'

'Five hundred francs wouldn't tempt you to let me have a free hand for just half an hour? I could do it, say somewhere short of Basle, and on reaching there make off. No one should be any the wiser, and they, the women, wouldn't dare to make a fuss.'

'It's I who do not dare — not for twice five hundred francs. My place is worth more than that; and if it is a dog's life, it is better than lying on the straw. Besides, there's her friend the Colonel, he'll be on the alert, you may depend.'

'So must I be, and I must find some way to

circumvent him. I'll be even with him. He shan't beat me, the overbearing, hectoring brute. It's between him and me, and I think I'm a match for him.'

I spoke this confidently to my friend, who engaged for his part to do all in his power to assist, or at least to do nothing against me, and I was content to bide my time. Pride goes before a fall. I was not as clever as I thought, and shall have to tell you how seriously I had underrated his worth in the coming trial of strength.

As the train sped on and the night began to close in on us, I remained quietly in my berth, pondering over my position, and in considering the course I should adopt under various contingencies. The first and most serious danger was that the lady should succeed in leaving the train at any of the intermediate stations at Basle, and so give me the slip. There were Laon, Rheims, Chaumont, and the rest.

It must be my business to keep close watch against any evasion of this kind, and Jules had promised to help. I did not look for any such attempt until far into the night, when the stations were empty and half-dark, and I agreed with Jules to divide the hours till daylight, he taking the first, I the last. We were due at Basle at 5 a.m., and I expected to join forces then with Tiler, my colleague, coming from the side of Ostend, via Brussels and Strasburg.

Meanwhile I kept quiet and made no sign beyond showing that I was there and on the spot ready to act if it should be necessary. Thus, when the train slackened speed on approaching a station, I was always on the move and the first to descend and patrol the platform. The Colonel always got out too, but he never accosted me; indeed, he seemed disposed to despise me, to ignore my existence, or dare me to the worst I could do.

I suppose the lady must have been of the same mind, for when dinner-time arrived, she came boldly out of her compartment, and I met her face to face for the first time, on her way to the restaurant. I was standing at the door of my compartment.

'Dinner is ready,' the Colonel said to me significantly, but I did not choose to understand, and shook my head, holding my ground.

'You are coming to dinner, I think,' he repeated in a sharp commanding way, as if he were talking to his soldiers.

'I shall please myself about that,' I replied gruffly.

'Not a bit of it. One moment,' he whispered to the lady, who walked on, and

52

turned again to me: 'Now see here, my friend, I do not mean to leave you behind. You will come to the dining-car with us, and no two ways about it, even if I have to carry you.'

'I won't dine with you,' I cried.

'I never asked you to dine with me, but you shall dine when I do. I will pay for your dinner, but I wouldn't sit at table with you for worlds,' he shouted with scornful laughter. 'You're going to dine under my eye, that's all, even though the sight of you is enough to make one sick. So come along, sharp's the word, see? Walk first; let him pass you, Mrs. Blair.'

I felt I had no choice. He was capable of again assaulting me. There was something in his manner that cowed me, and I was obliged in spite of myself to give way.

There were only three of us in the dining-car, and we were not a very merry company. Our tables were laid almost adjoining, and there was no conversation between us, except when the Colonel asked me with contemptuous civility what wine I preferred. He did not talk to the lady, or the merest commonplaces, for I was within earshot. But I made an excellent dinner, I must confess. I had eaten nothing since Amiens. Then I got back to my berth, where the bed was made. I threw myself on to it,

53

rejoiced at the prospect of getting a few hours' sleep while Jules remained on the watch.

He was to call me a little before reaching Basle, and, like an ass that I was, I fully relied on his doing so, believing him to be my friend. Such friendship as his did not bear any great strain, as I learnt presently to my great chagrin.

I slept heavily, but in fitful snatches, as a man does when constantly disturbed by the whirr and whizzing of the train, the rattle and jangle of wheels passing over ill-jointed points. After one of the longest periods of unconsciousness I awoke, aroused by the complete absence of noise. The train was at a standstill in some station and making a very protracted halt.

Something moved me to lift the blind and look out, and I saw, not without uneasiness, that we were at Basle. I thought I recognized the station, but I soon made out for certain the name 'Basilea' (Basle), and saw the clock with the fingers at five-thirty. People were already on the move, work-people, the thrifty, industrious Swiss, forestalling time, travellers in twos and threes arriving and departing by the early train through this great junction on the frontier of Switzerland.

Stay! What? Who are those crossing the

platform hurriedly. Great powers! Right under my eyes, a little party of four, two females, two men accompanying them, escorting them, carrying rugs and parcels. There could not be a shadow of doubt.

It was the lady, the so-called Mrs. Blair, in full flight, with all her belongings, and under the care and guidance not only of the Colonel, that of course, but also of the perfidious Jules l'Echelle. He had sold me! All doubt of his treachery disappeared when on rushing to the door I found I had been locked into my compartment.

I rang the electric bell frantically, again and again. I got no answer; I threw up the window and thrust my head out, shouting for help, but got none, only one or two sluggish porters came up and asked what was amiss, answering stolidly, when they heard, that it was none of their business. 'They had no key, it must be a mistake. The conductor would explain, I must wait till he came.'

Presently Jules arrived, walking very leisurely from the direction of the restaurant, and he stood right under my window with a grin on his face and mockery in his voice.

'What's wrong? Locked in? Can't be possible? Who could have done it? I will inquire,' he said slowly and imperturbably.

'No, no; let me out first. You can do it if

you choose. I believe it was your trickery from the first. I must get out, I tell you, or they will escape me,' I cried.

'Not unlikely. I may say it is pretty certain they will. That was the Colonel's idea; you'd better talk to him about it next time you see him.'

'And that will be never, I expect. He's not going to show up here again.'

'There you're wrong; he will be back before the train starts, you may rely on that, and you'll be able to talk to him. We'll let you out then,' he was laughing at me, traitor that he was. 'Here he comes. We're just going on.'

Now I saw my last chance of successfully performing my mission disappearing beyond recall. I renewed my shouts and protests, but was only laughed at for my pains. The railway officials at Basle might have interfered, but Jules answered for me, declaring with a significant gesture that I was in drink and that he would see to me.

I quite despaired. Already the train was moving out of the station, when, to my intense joy, I caught sight of Ludovic Tiler, who came down the platform running alongside us, and crying, 'Falfani, Falfani,' as he recognized me.

'Don't mind me,' I shouted to him. 'I must go on, I can't help myself. It's for you to take it up now. She's in the restaurant. You'll easily know her, in a long ulster, with her maid and the child. You can't miss her. By the Lord, she is standing at the door! Get away with you, don't let her see you talking with me. She must not know we are acting in common, and I do hope she hasn't noticed. Be off, I tell you, only let me hear of you; wire to Lucerne what you're doing. Address telegraph-office. Send me a second message at Goeschenen. I shall get one or both. Say where I may answer and where I can join you.'

8

The timely appearance of my colleague, Ludovic Tiler, consoled me a little for the loss of the lady and her lot. I had failed, myself, but I hoped that with my lead he would get on to the scent and keep to it. Ere long, on the first intimation from him I might come into the game again. I should be guided by his wire if I got it.

For the moment I was most concerned to find out whether Tiler's intervention and my short talk with him had been noticed by the other side. If the Colonel knew that another man was on his friend's track, he would surely have left the train at once so as to go to her assistance. But he was still in the train, I could hear him plainly, speaking to Jules in the next compartment. Again, as we sped on, I reasoned favourably from their leaving me as I was, still under lock and key. No one came near me until after we had passed Olten station, the first stopping-place after Basle, where I could alight and retrace my steps. By holding on to me I guessed that I was still thought to be the chief danger, and that they had no suspicion of Tiler's existence.

I laughed in my sleeve, but not the less did I rage and storm when Jules l'Echelle came with the Colonel to release me.

'You shall pay for this,' I cried hotly.

'As for you, l'Echelle, it shall cost you your place, and I'll take the law of you, Colonel Annesley; I'll get damages and you shall answer for your illegal action.'

'Pfui!' retorted the Colonel. 'The mischief you can do is nothing to what you might have done. We can stand the racket. I've bested you for the present — that's the chief thing, anyway. You can't persecute the poor lady any more.'

'Poor lady! Do you know who she is or was, anyway?'

'Of course I do,' he answered bold as brass.

'Did she let on? Told you, herself? My word! She's got a nerve. I wonder she'd own to it after all she's done.'

'Silence!' he shouted, in a great taking. 'If you dare to utter a single word against that lady, I'll break every bone in your body.'

'I'm saying nothing — it's not me, it's all the world. It was in the papers, you must have read them, the most awful story, such — such depravity there never was — such treachery, such gross misconduct.'

He caught me by the arm so violently and looked so fierce that for a moment I was quite alarmed.

'Drop it, I tell you. Leave the lady alone, both by word and deed. You'll never find her again, I've seen to that. She has escaped you.'

'Aha! You think so? Don't be too cocksure. We understand our business better than that, we don't go into it single-handed. You've collared me for a bit, but I'm not the only one in the show.'

'The only one that counts,' he said sneering.

'Am I?' I answered in the same tone. 'What if I had a pal waiting for me at Basle, who received my instructions there — just when you thought you had me safe — and has now taken up the running?'

He was perfectly staggered at this, I could see plainly. I thought at first he would have struck me, he was so much upset.

'You infernal villain,' he shouted, 'I believe the whole thing is a confounded lie! Explain.'

'I owe you no explanations,' I replied stiffly, 'my duty is to my employers. I only account to them for my conduct. I am a confidential agent.'

He seemed impressed by this, for when he spoke again it was more quietly. But he looked me very straight in the eyes. I felt that he was still likely to give trouble.

'Well, I suppose I cannot expect you to tell me things. You must go your own way and I shall go mine.'

'I should advise you to leave it, Colonel,' I said, civilly enough. 'I'm always anxious to conciliate and avoid unpleasantness. Give up the whole business; you will only burn your fingers.'

'Ah! How so?'

'The law is altogether against you. It is a nasty job; better not be mixed up in it. Have you any idea what that woman — that lady,' I corrected myself, for his eyes flashed, 'has done?'

'Nothing really wrong,' he was warming up into a new burst of passion.

'Tell that to the Courts and to the Judge when you are prosecuted for contempt and charged as an accessory after the fact. How will you like that? It will take the starch out of you.'

'Rot! The law can't do us much harm. The only person who might make it disagreeable is Lord Blackadder, and I snap my fingers at him.'

'The Earl of Blackadder? Are you mad? He is a great personage, a rich and powerful nobleman. You cannot afford to fight him; he will be too strong for you. He has been made the victim of an abominable outrage, and will spare no effort, no means, no money to recover his own.'

'Lord Blackadder is a cad — a cruel,

cowardly ruffian. I know all about him and what has happened. It would give me the greatest pleasure to kick him down the street. Failing that, I shall do my best to upset and spoil his schemes, and so you know.'

I smiled contemptuously. 'A mere Colonel against an Earl! What sort of a chance have you? It's too absurd.'

'We shall see. Those laugh longest who laugh last.'

By this time our talk was done, for we were approaching Lucerne, and I began to think over my next plans. All must depend on what I heard there — upon what news, if any, came from Ludovic Tiler.

So on my arrival I made my way straight to the telegraph-office in the corner of the great station, and on showing my card an envelope was handed to me. It was from Tiler at Basle, and ran as follows:

'They have booked through by 7.30 a.m., via Brienne, Lausanne to Brieg, and I suppose the Simplon. I shall accompany. Can you join me at either end — Brieg or Domo Dossola? The sooner the better. Wire me from all places along the route, giving your movements. Address me in my train No. 70.'

The news pointed pretty clearly to the passage of the Alps and descent into Italy by another route than the St. Gothard. I had my

Bradshaw in my bag, and proceeded at once to verify the itinerary by the time-table, while I drank my early coffee in the restaurant upon the station platform. I was most anxious to join hands with Tiler, and quickly turned over the leaves of my railway guide to see if it was possible, and how it might best be managed.

My first idea was to retrace my steps to Basle and follow him by the same road. But I soon found that the trains would not fit in the very least. He would be travelling by the one fast train in the day, which was due at Brieg at four o'clock in the afternoon. My first chance, if I caught the very next train back from Lucerne, would only get me to Brieg by the eleven o'clock the following morning.

It was not good enough, and I dismissed the idea forthwith. Then I remembered that by getting off the St. Gothard railway at Goeschenen I should strike the old Furka diligence route by the Devil's Bridge, Hospenthal, and the Rhone Glacier, a drive of fifty miles, more or less, but at least it would get me to Brieg that same night by 10 or 11 o'clock.

Before adopting this line I had to consider that there was a risk of missing Tiler and his quarry; that is to say, of being too late for them; for the lady might decide to push on directly she reached Brieg, taking a special carriage extra post as far as the Simplon at least, even into Domo Dossola. She was presumably in such a hurry that the night journey would hardly deter her from driving over the pass. Tiler would certainly follow. By the time I reached Brieg they would be halfway across the Alps, and I must take the same road, making a stern chase, proverbially the longest.

I turned my attention, therefore, to the Italian end of the carriage road, and to seeing how and when I could reach Domo Dossola, the alternative suggestion made by Tiler. There would be no difficulty as to that, and I found I could be there in good time the same evening. I worked it out on the tables and it looked easy enough.

Leave Lucerne by the St. Gothard railway, pass Goeschenen, and go through the tunnel down the Italian side as far as Bellizona. Thence a branch line would take me to Locarno and into touch with the steamboat service on Lake Maggiore. There was a fixed connection according to the tables, and I should land at Pallanza within a short hour's drive of the line to Domo Dossola. I could be established there by nightfall and would command the situation. Every carriage that came down the Simplon must come under my eye.

There could be no doubt that the Bellizona-Locarno Lake line was the preferable one, and I finally decided in favour of it. I closed my Bradshaw with a bang, replaced it in my bag, drank up my coffee, and started for the telegraph office. I meant to advise Tiler of my plans, and at the same time arrange with him to look out for me just outside the terminus station at Domo Dossola, or to communicate with me there at the Hôtel de la Poste.

On coming out I ran up against the last person I wished to see. It was the Colonel, who greeted me with a loud laugh, and gave me a slap on the back.

'Halloa, my wily detective,' he said mockingly; 'settled it all quite to your satisfaction? Done with Bradshaw — sent off your wires? Well, what's the next move?'

'I decline to hold any conversation with you,' I began severely. 'I beg you will not intrude upon my privacy. I do not desire your acquaintance.'

'Hoity toity!' he cried. 'On your high horse, eh? Aren't you afraid you may fall off or get knocked off?' and he raised his hand with an ugly gesture.

'We are not alone now in a railway carriage. There are police about, and the Swiss police do not approve of brawling,' I replied, with all the dignity I could assume.

'Come, Falfani, tell me what you mean to do now,' he went on in the same tone.

'Your questions are an impertinence. I do not know you. I do not choose to know you, and I beg you will leave me alone.'

'Don't think of it, my fine fellow. I'm not going to leave you alone. You may make up your mind to that. Where you go, I go; what you do, I shall do. We are inseparables, you and I, as much united as the Siamese twins. So I tell you.'

'But it's monstrous, it's not to be tolerated. I shall appeal for protection to the authorities.'

'Do so, my friend, do so. See which will get the best of that. I don't want to swagger, but at any rate all the world knows pretty well who I am; but what shall you call yourself, Mr. Falfani?'

'I have my credentials from my employers; I have letters, testimonials, recommendations from the best people.'

'Including the Earl of Blackadder, I presume? I admit your great advantages. Well, try it. You may get the best of it in the long run, but you'll lose a good deal of time. I'm not in a hurry,' he said with emphasis, and promptly recalled me to my senses, for I realized that I could not fight him that way. It must be by stratagem or evasion. I must throw dust in his eyes, put him off the scent, mislead, befool, elude him somehow.

How was I to shake him off now I saw that he was determined to stick to me? He had said it in so many words. He would not let me out of his sight; wherever I went he was coming too.

The time was drawing on for the departure of the St. Gothard express at 9.08 a.m., and as yet I had no ticket. I had booked at Amiens as far as Lucerne only, leaving further plans as events might fall out. Now I desired to go on, but did not see how I was to take a fresh ticket without his learning my destination. He would be certain to be within earshot when I went up to the window.

I was beginning to despair when I saw Cook's man, who was, as usual, hovering about to assist travellers in trouble, and I beckoned him to approach.

'See that gentleman,' I nodded towards the Colonel. 'He wants you; do your best for him.' And when the tourist agent proceeded on his mission to be accosted, I fear rather unceremoniously, I slipped off and hid out of sight.

I felt sure I was unobserved as I took my place in the crowd at the ticket-window, but when I had asked and paid for my place to

Locarno I heard, to my disgust, some one else applying for a ticket to exactly the same place, and in a voice that was strangely familiar.

On looking round I saw Jules l'Echelle, the sleeping-car conductor, but out of uniform, and with an amused grin on his face.

'It seems that we are still to be fellow travellers,' he observed casually.

'What is taking you to Lake Maggiore? How about your service on the car?' I asked suspiciously.

'I have business at Locarno, and have got a few days' leave to attend to it.'

I felt he was lying to me. He had been bought, I was sure. His business was the Colonel's, who had set him to assist in watching me. I had two enemies then to encounter, and I realized with some misgiving that the Colonel was not a man to be despised.

9

I secured a place with difficulty; there was rather a rush for the St. Gothard express when it ran in. It was composed as usual of corridor carriages, all classes *en suite*, and I knew that it would be impossible to conceal the fact that I was on board the train. Within five minutes Jules had verified the fact and taken seats in the immediate neighbourhood, to which he and the Colonel presently came.

'Quite a pleasant little party!' he said in a bantering tone. 'All bound for Locarno, eh? Ever been to Locarno before, Mr. Falfani? Delightful lake, Maggiore. Many excursions, especially by steamer; the Borromean islands well worth seeing, and Baveno and Stresa and the road to the Simplon.'

I refused to be drawn, and only muttered that I hated excursions and steamers and lakes, and wished to be left in peace.

'A little out of sorts, I'm afraid, Mr. Falfani. Sad that. Too many emotions, want of sleep, perhaps. You *would* do *too* much last night.' He still kept up his hateful babble, and Jules maddened me by his sniggering enjoyment of my discomfiture.

More than ever did I set my brain to puzzle out some way of escaping this horrible infliction. Was it not possible to give them the slip, somehow, somewhere? I took the Colonel's hint, and pretended to take refuge in sleep, and at last, I believe, I dozed off. It must have been in my dreams that an idea came to me, a simple idea, easy of execution with luck and determination.

It was suggested to me by the short tunnels that succeed so frequently in the ascent of the St. Gothard Alps. They are, as most people know, a chief feature in the mountain railway, and a marvel of engineering skill, being cut in circles to give the necessary length and gain the height with a moderate gradient. Speed is so far slackened that it would be quite possible to drop off the train without injury whenever inclined. My only difficulty would be to alight without interference from my persecutors.

I nursed my project with eyes shut, still feigning sleep; and my extreme quiescence had, as I hoped, the effect of throwing them off their guard. Jules, like all in the same employment, was always ready for forty winks, and I saw that he was sound and snoring just as we entered the last tunnel before reaching the entrance of the final great tunnel at Goeschenen. I could not be quite sure of the Colonel, but his attitude was that of a man resting, and who had very nearly lost himself, if he had not quite gone off.

Now was my time. If it was to be done at all it must be quickly, instantaneously almost. Fortunately we sat at the extreme end of a coach, in the last places, and besides we three there was only one other occupant in the compartment of six. The fourth passenger was awake, but I made a bid for his good-will by touching my lips with a finger, and the next minute I was gone.

I expected to hear the alarm given at my disappearance, but none reached my ears, as the train rattled past me with its twinkling lights and noisy road. I held myself close against the side of the tunnel in perfect safety, although the hot wind of the passing cars fanned my cheek and rather terrified me. The moment the train was well gone I faced the glimmering light that showed the entrance to the tunnel at the further end from the station, and ran to it with all speed.

I knew that my jump from the train could not pass unnoticed, and I counted on being followed. I expected that the tunnel would be explored by people from Goeschenen so soon as the train ran in and reported. My first object, therefore, was to quit the line, and I did so directly I was clear of the tunnel. I climbed the fence, dropped into a road, left that again to ascend the slope and take shelter among the rocks and trees.

The pursuit, if any, was not very keen or long maintained. When all was quiet, an hour later I made for the highroad, the famous old road that leads through the Devil's Pass to Andermatt, three miles above. I altogether avoided the Goeschenen station, fearing any inconvenient inquiries, and abandoned all idea of getting the telegram from Tiler that might be possibly awaiting me. It did not much matter. I should be obliged now to send him fresh news, news of the changed plans that took me direct into Brieg; and on entering Andermatt I came upon the post-office, just where I wanted it, both to send my message and order an extra post carriage from Brieg.

It was with a sense of intense relief that I sank back into the cushions and felt that at last I was free. My satisfaction was abruptly destroyed. Long before I reached Hospenthal, a mile or so from Andermatt, I was disturbed by strange cries to the accompaniment of harness bells.

'Yo-icks, Yo-icks, G-o-ne away!' was borne after me with all the force of stentorian lungs, and looking round I saw to my horror a second carriage coming on at top speed, and beyond all question aiming to overtake us. Soon they drew nearer, near enough for speech, and the accursed Colonel hailed me.

'Why, you cunning fox, so you broke cover and got away all in a moment! Lucky you were seen leaving the train, or we might have overrun the scent and gone on.'

I did not answer.

'Nice morning for a drive, Mr. Falfani, and a long drive,' he went on, laughing boisterously. 'Going all the way to Brieg by road, I believe? So are we. Pity we did not join forces. One carriage would have done for all three of us.'

Still I did not speak.

'A bit ugly, eh? Don't fuss, man. It's all in the day's work.'

With that I desired my driver to pull up, and waved my hand to the others, motioning to them that the road was theirs.

But when I stopped they stopped, and the Colonel jeered. When I drove on they came along too, laughing. We did this several times; and when at the two roads just through Hospenthal, one by the St. Gothard, the other leading to the Furka, I took the first for a short distance, then turned back, just to try my pursuers. They still stuck to me. My heart sank within me. I was in this accursed soldier's claws. He had collared me, he was on my back, and I felt that I must throw up the sponge.

'I gave you fair notice that you would not get rid of me, and by heaven you shall not,' he cried fiercely, putting off all at once the lighter mockery of his tone. 'I know what is taking you to Brieg. You think to find your confederate there, and you hope that, combined, the two of you will get the better of that lady. You shan't, not if I can prevent you by any means in my power; understand that, and look out for squalls if you try.'

I confess he cowed me; he was so strong, so masterful, and, as I began to fear, so unscrupulous, that I felt I could not make head against him. Certainly not alone. I must have Tiler's help, his counsel, countenance, active support. I must get in touch with him at the earliest possible moment and my nearest way to him, situated as I was now, must be at or through Brieg.

So I resigned myself to my fate, and suffered myself to be driven on with my pertinacious escort hanging on to me mile after mile of my wearing and interminable journey. We pulled up for luncheon and a short rest at the Furka; again in the afternoon at the Rhone Glacier. Then we pursued our way all along the valley, with the great snow peak of the Matterhorn in front of us, through village and hamlet, in the fast fading light, and so on under the dark but luminous sky into Munster, Fiesch, and Morel, till at length we rolled into Brieg about 11 p.m.

I drove straight to the Hôtel de la Poste, careless that my tormentors were accompanying me; they could do me no more harm, and Tiler was at hand to help in vindicating our position.

There was no Tiler at the Hôtel de la Poste; no Tiler in Brieg. Only a brief telegram from him conveying unwelcome and astounding intelligence. It had been despatched from Vevey about 2 p.m., and it said:

'Lost her somewhere between this and Lausanne. Am trying back. Shall wire you again to Brieg. Wait there or leave address.'

My face must have betrayed my abject despair. I was so completely knocked over that I offered no opposition when the Colonel impudently took the telegram out of my hand and read it coolly.

'Drawn blank!' he cried, unable to contain himself for joy. 'By the Lord Harry, that's good.'

10

The Statement of the Second Detective, Ludovic Tiler

I travelled via Ostend, Brussels and Strasburg, and was due at Basle from that side at 4.35 a.m. My instructions were to look out for Falfani there, and thought I might do so if our train was fairly punctual, as it was. We were 'on time,' and the answer to my first question was that the Lucerne express was still at the platform, but on the point of departure.

I got one glimpse of Falfani and one word with him. He was in trouble himself; they had nipped him, caught him tight, and thrown him off the scent. I was now to take up the running.

'You've got your chance now, Ludovic,' he said hurriedly, as he leaned out of the carriage window. 'I'm not jealous, as you often are, but it's deuced hard on me. Anyhow, stick to her like wax, and keep your eyes skinned. She's got the wiles of the devil, and will sell you like a dog if you don't mind. Hurry now; you'll pick her up in the waiting-room or restaurant, and can't miss her.'

He gave me the description, and I left him, promising him a wire at the telegraph office, Lucerne. He was right, there was no mistaking her. Few people were about at that time in the morning, and there was not a soul among the plain-headed, commonplace Swiss folk to compare with her, an English lady with her belongings.

She was quite a beauty, tall, straight, lissom, in her tight-fitting ulster; her piquante-looking heather cap perched on chestnut curls, and setting off as handsome a face as I have ever seen. And I have seen and admired many, for I don't deny that I've a strong penchant for pretty women, and this was the pick of the basket. It was rather a bore to be put on to her in the way of business; but why should I not get a little pleasure out of it if I could? I need not be disagreeable; it might help matters and pass the time pleasantly, even if in the end I might have to show my teeth.

I saw her looking me over as I walked into the waiting-room, curiously, critically, and for a moment I fancied she guessed who I was. Had she seen me talking to Falfani?

If so — if she thought me one of her persecutors — she would hardly look upon me without repugnance, yet I almost believed it was all the other way. I had an idea that she did not altogether dislike me, that she was pleased with my personal appearance. Why not? I had had my successes in my time, and may say, although it sounds conceited, that I had won the approval of other ladies quite as high-toned. By and by it might be my unpleasant duty to be disagreeable. In the meantime it would be amusing, enjoyable, to make friends.

So far I had still to ascertain the direction in which she was bound. She had taken her ticket. That might be safely inferred, for she was in the waiting-room with her porter and her bags, ready to pass out upon the platform as soon as the doors were opened. (Everyone knows that the idiotic and uncomfortable practice still prevails in Switzerland of shutting passengers off from the train till the very last moment.)

This waiting-room served for many lines, and I could only wait patiently to enter the particular train for which she would be summoned. When at length an official unlocked the door and announced the train for Biel, Neuchâtel, Lausanne, and Brieg, she got up to take her seat, and I had no longer any doubt as to the direction of her journey. So as I saw her go, I slipped back to the ticket-office and took my place all the way to

Brieg, the furthest point on the line. This was obviously my best and safest plan, as I should then be ready for anything that happened. I could get out anywhere, wherever she did, in fact. After getting my ticket I found time to telegraph to Falfani at Lucerne, giving him my latest news, and then proceeded to the train.

I found the lady easily enough, and got into the same carriage with her. It was one of those on the Swiss plan, with many compartments opening into one another *en suite*. Although the seat I chose was at a discreet distance, I was able to keep her in view.

I was wondering whether it would be possible for me to break the ice and make her acquaintance, when luck served me better than I dared to hope. One of the Swiss guards of the train, a surly, overbearing brute, like so many others of his class, accosted her rudely, and from his gestures was evidently taking her to task as to the number and size of her parcels in the net above. He began to shift them, and, despite her indignant protests in imperfect German, threw some of them on the floor.

This was my opportunity. I hurried to the rescue, and, being fluent in German as in several other languages — it is part of my stock in trade — I sharply reproved the guard and called him an unmannerly boor for his cowardly treatment of an unprotected lady. My reward was a sweet smile, and I felt encouraged to hazard a few words in reply to her cordial thanks. She responded quickly, readily, and I thought I might improve the occasion by politely inquiring if I could be of any further service to her.

'Perhaps you can tell me, you see I am strange on this line,' she answered with a perfectly innocent air, 'do you happen to know at what time we are due at Lausanne?'

'Not to the minute,' I replied. 'I have a railway guide in my bag, shall I fetch it?'

'No, no, I should not like to give you so much trouble.'

'But it will be no trouble. Let me fetch my bag.'

I went off in perfect good faith, anxious to oblige so charming a lady. I had not the slightest suspicion that she was playing with me. Silly ass that I was, I failed to detect the warning that dropped from her own lips.

When I got back with the Bradshaw I came upon them for just one moment unawares. The maid must have been making some remarks displeasing to my lady, who was answering her with much asperity.

'I know what I am doing, Philpotts. Be so

good as to leave it to me. It is the only way.'

Then she caught sight of me as I stood before her, and her manner instantly changed. She addressed me very sweetly and with the utmost composure. 'Oh, how very good of you, I feel quite ashamed of myself.'

'Why should you? It is delightful to be of use to you. Lausanne I think you said?' I asked casually as I turned over the pages of the guide. 'You are going to Lausanne?'

'No, Vevey to Montreux. I only wanted to know whether there would be time for *déjeuner* at Lausanne. I think there is no dining-car on this train?'

'No, it is on the next, which is extraordinarily bad mismanagement. It is a slow train the next, and we are a special express. But you will have a clear half-hour to spare at Lausanne. That will be enough, I presume? Lausanne at 12 noon, and we go on at half-past.'

'You, too, are going beyond Lausanne?'

'Possibly, I am not quite sure. It depends upon my meeting friends somewhere on the lake, either there or further on. If they come on board we shall run on to Brieg so as to drop over the Alps to Lake Maggiore by the Simplon route.'

I threw this out carelessly but with deliberate intention, and the shot told. A

81

crimson flush came over her face and her hands trembled violently. I had not the smallest doubt that this was her plan also. She was bound to cross over into Italy, that we knew, or our employers firmly believed it, and as she had been driven off the St. Gothard by Falfani she had now doubled back by Switzerland to make the journey to Brieg and across the mountains by road.

I had scored as I thought, but I forgot that in gaining the knowledge I had betrayed my own intentions, and put her upon her guard. I was to pay for this.

'Oh, really,' she said quietly and with polite interest, having entirely recovered her composure. 'I dare say a very pleasant drive. How long does it take, have you any idea, and how do you travel?'

'It is about nine hours by diligence,' I said, consulting the Bradshaw, 'and the fare is forty francs, but by private carriage or extra post a good deal more.'

'May I look?' and I handed her the book, 'although I never could understand Bradshaw,' she added pleasantly.

'I shall be very pleased to explain if you are in doubt,' I suggested; but she declined laughingly, saying it would amuse her to puzzle out things, so I left her the book and composed myself into a corner while the train rattled on. I mused and dozed and dreamily watched her pretty face admiringly, as she pored over the pages of the Guide, little thinking she was perfecting a plan for my undoing.

The first stop was at Biel or Bienne, its French name, and there was a halt of ten minutes or more. I made my way to the telegraph office in the station, where to my great satisfaction I found a message from Falfani, informing me that he should make the best of his way to Brieg, unless I could suggest something better.

The answer I despatched at once to Goeschenen was worded as follows: 'Declares she is going to Montreux only. Believe untrue. Still think her destination Brieg. Come on there anyhow and await further from me. May be necessary to join forces.' We were in accord, Falfani and I, and in communication.

I was well satisfied with what we were doing, and on receiving the second and third telegrams at Neuchâtel and Yverdun I was all the more pleased. At last we were nearing Lausanne, and I looked across to my lady to prepare her for getting out. I had no need to attract her attention, for I caught her eyes fixed on me and believe she was watching me furtively. The smile that came upon her lips was so pleasant and sweet that it might have overjoyed a more conceited man than myself.

'Are we near then? Delightful! I never was so hungry in my life,' and the smile expanded into a gay laugh as she rose to her feet and was ready to leave the carriage.

'I'm afraid you will have to wait, Philpotts, we cannot leave that,' she pointed to the child nestling sound asleep by her side. 'But I will send or bring you something. This gentleman will perhaps escort me to the refreshment-room.'

I agreed, of course, and saying, 'Only too charmed,' I led the way — a long way, for the restaurant is at the far end of the platform. At last we sat down *tête-à-tête* and prepared to do full justice to the meal. Strange to say, despite her anticipations, she proved to have very little appetite.

'I must have waited too long,' she said, as she trifled with a cutlet. 'I shall perhaps like something else better,' and she went carefully through the whole *menu*, so that the time slipped away, and we were within five minutes of departure.

'And poor dear Philpotts, I had quite forgotten her. Come and help me choose,' and in duty bound I gallantly carried the food back to the train.

I walked ahead briskly, and making my way

to the places where we had left the maid and child, jumped in.

They were gone, the two of them. Everything was gone, rugs, bags, belongings, people. The seats were empty, and as the compartment was quite empty, too, no one could tell me when they had left or where they had gone.

I turned quickly round to my companion, who was, I thought, following close at my heels, and found to my utter amazement that she also had disappeared.

11

For the moment I was dazed and dumfounded, but I took a pull on myself quickly. It was a clever plant. Had they sold me completely? That was still to be seen. My one chance was in prompt action; I must hunt them up, recover trace of them with all possible despatch, follow them, and find them wherever they might be.

There was just the chance that they had only moved into another carriage, thinking that when I missed them I should get out and hunt for them in the station. To counter that I ran up and down the train, in and out of the carriages, questing like a hound, searching everywhere. So eager was I that I neglected the ordinary warnings that the train was about to start; the guard's *fertig* ('ready'), the sounding horn, the answering engine whistle, I overlooked them all, and we moved on before I could descend. I made as though to jump off hastily, but was prevented.

'*Was ist das? Nein, nein, verboten.*' A hand caught me roughly by the collar and dragged me back. It was the enemy I had made in championing my lady, the guard of the train, who gladly seized the chance of being disagreeable to me.

I fought hard to be free, but by the time I had shaken him off the speed had so increased that it would have been unsafe to leave the train. I had no choice but to go on, harking back as soon as I could. Fortunately our first stop was within five and twenty minutes, at Vevey; and there in ten minutes more I found a train back to Lausanne, so that I had lost less than an hour and a half in all.

But much may happen in that brief space of time. It was more than enough for my fugitives to clear out of the Lausanne station and make some new move, to hide away in an out-of-the-way spot, go to ground in fact, or travel in another direction.

My first business was to inquire in and about the station for a person or persons answering to the parties I missed. Had they separated, these two women, for good and all? That was most unlikely. If the maid had gone off first, I had to consider whether they would not again join forces as soon as I was well out of the way. They would surely feel safer, happier, together, and this encouraged me to ask first for two people, two females, a lady and her servant, one of them, the latter, carrying a child.

There were many officials about in uniform, and all alike supercilious and indifferent, after the manner of their class, to the travelling public, and I could get none to take the smallest interest in my affairs. One shrugged his shoulders, another stared at me in insolent silence, a third answered me abruptly that he was too occupied to bother himself, and a fourth peremptorily ordered me not to hang any longer about the station.

Foiled thus by the railway staff — and I desire to place on record here my deliberate opinion after many years' experience in many lands, that for rudeness and overbearing manners the Swiss functionary has no equal in the whole world — I went outside the station and sought information among the cabmen and touts who hang about waiting to take up travellers. I accosted all the drivers patiently one by one, but could gather nothing definite from any of them. Most had been on the stand at the arrival of the midday train, many had been engaged to convey passengers and baggage up into the town of Lausanne, and had deposited their fares at various hotels and private residences, but no one had driven any party answering to those of whom I was in search.

This practically decided the point that my lady had not left the station in a carriage or openly, if she had walked. But that she had not been observed did not dispose of the question. They were dull, stupid men, these, only intent on their own business, who would pay little attention to humble persons on foot showing no desire to hire a cab. I would not be baffled thus soon in my quest. A confidential agent who will not take infinite pains in his researches had better seek some other line of business. As I stood there in front of the great station belonging to the Jura-Simplon, I saw facing me a small façade of the Gare Sainte Luce, one of the intermediate stations on the *Ficelle* or cable railway that connects Ouchy on the lake with Lausanne above.

It was not a hundred yards distant; it could be easily and quickly reached, and without much observation, if a person waited till the immediate neighbourhood had been cleared by the general exodus after the arrival of the chief express of the day. There were any number of trains by this *funiculaire* — at every half-hour indeed — and any one taking this route could reach either Lausanne or Ouchy after a very few minutes' journey up or down. To extend my investigation on that side was of obvious and pressing importance. I was only too conscious of my great loss of time, now at the outset, which might efface all tracks and cut me off hopelessly from any clue.

I was soon across and inside the Sainte

Luce station, but still undecided which direction I should choose, when the little car arrived going upward, and I ran over to that platform and jumped in. I must begin one way or the other, and I proceeded at once to question the conductor, when he nicked my ticket, only to draw perfectly blank.

'Have I seen two ladies and a child this morning? But, grand Dieu, I have seen two thousand. It is idiote to ask such questions, monsieur, of a busy man.'

'I can pay for what I want,' I whispered gently, as I slipped a five-franc piece into his hand, ever mindful of the true saying, Point d'argent, point de Suisse; and the bribe entirely changed his tone.

'A lady, handsome, tall, distinguished, comme il faut, with a companion, a servant, a nurse carrying a child?' He repeated my description, adding, 'Parfaitement, I saw her. She was not one to forget quickly.'

'And she was going to Lausanne?'

'Ma foi, yes, I believe so; or was it to Ouchy?' He seemed overwhelmed with sudden doubt. 'Lausanne or Ouchy? Up or down? Twenty thousand thunders, but I cannot remember, not — ' he dropped his voice — 'not for five francs.'

I doubled the dose, and hoped I had now sufficiently stimulated his memory or unloosed his tongue. But the rascal was still hesitating when we reached the top, and I could get nothing more than that it was certainly Lausanne, 'if,' he added cunningly, 'it was not Ouchy.' But he had seen her, that was sure — seen her that very day upon the line, not more than an hour or two before. He had especially admired her; *dame!* he had an eye for the *beau sexe*; and yet more he noticed that she talked English, of which he knew some words, to her maid. But whether she was bound to Lausanne or Ouchy, '*diable*, who could say?'

I had got little in return for my ten francs expended on this ambiguous news, but now that I found myself actually in Lausanne I felt that it behoved me to scour the city for traces of my quarry. She might not have come here at all, yet there was an even chance the other way, and I should be mad not to follow the threads I held in my hand. I resolved to inquire at all the hotels forthwith. It would take time and trouble, but it was essential. I must run her to ground if possible, fix her once more, or I should never again dare to look my employers in the face. I was ashamed to confess to Falfani that I had been outwitted and befooled. I would send him no more telegrams until I had something more satisfactory to say.

I was now upon the great bridge that spans the valley of the Flon and joins the old with the new quarter of Lausanne. The best hotels, the Gibbon, Richemont, Falcon, Grand Pont, and several more, stood within easy reach, and I soon exhausted this branch of the inquiry. I found a *valet de place* hanging about the Gibbon, whose services I secured, and instructed him to complete the investigation, extending it to all the minor hotels and pensions, some half-dozen more, reserving to myself the terminus by the great station, which I had overlooked when leaving for the *Ficelle* or cable railway. I meant to wait for him there to hear his report, but at the same time I took his address — Eugène Falloon, Rue Pré Fleuri — where I could give him an appointment in case I missed him at the terminus. He was a long, lean, hungry-looking fellow, clumsily made, with an enormous head and misshapen hands and feet; but he was no fool this Falloon, and his local knowledge proved exceedingly useful.

On entering the car for the journey down I came upon the conductor who had been of so little use to me, and I was about to upbraid him when he disarmed me by volunteering fresh news.

'Ah, but, monsieur, I know much better now. I recollect exactly. The lady with her people certainly went down, for I have seen a porter who helped her with her effects from the line to the steamboat pier at Ouchy.'

'And on board the steamer? Going in which direction?' I asked eagerly.

'He shall tell you himself if I can find him when we reach the terminus. It may not be easy, but I could do it if — '

Another and a third five-franc piece solved his doubts, and I abandoned my visit to the terminus hotel to seize this more tangible clue, and proceeded at once to the lake shore.

12

On reaching the steamboat pier I was introduced to the porter, a shock-headed, stupid-looking creature, whom I forthwith questioned eagerly; but elicited only vague and, I felt sure, misleading replies. The conductor assisted at my interview, stimulating and encouraging the man to speak, and overdid it, as I thought. I strongly suspected that this new evidence had been produced in order to bleed me further. Had he really seen this English lady? Would he describe her appearance to me, and that of her companion? Was she tall or short? Well dressed, handsome, or the reverse? What was her companion like? Tall or short? How dressed, and did he suppose her condition to be that of a lady like the other, equal in rank, or an inferior?

The answers I got were not encouraging. Ladies? Of course they were ladies, both of them. Dressed? In the very latest fashion. They were very distinguished people.

'Were they carrying anything, either of them?' I inquired.

'Yes, when I saw them first they had much

94

baggage. It was for that they summoned me. Handbags, *sacs de nuit*, rugs, wrappers, bonnet-boxes, many things, like all travellers.'

'And you noticed nothing big, no parcel for which they were particularly concerned?'

'They were anxious about everything, and worried me about everything, but about no one thing especially that I can remember.'

This did not tally with my own observation and the extreme care taken of the child in the woman's arms. I began to believe that my friend was a humbug and could tell me nothing of his own knowledge.

'What time was it?' I went on.

'Some hours ago. I did not look at the clock.'

'But you know by the steamers that arrive. You men must know which are due, and when they pass through.'

'Come, come, Antoine,' broke in the conductor, determined to give him a lead, 'you must know that; there are not so many. It would be about 2 p.m., wouldn't it, when the express boat comes from Vevey and Bouveret?'

'Yes, I make no doubt of that,' said the man, with a gleam of intelligence upon his stolid face.

'And the ladies went on board it, you say? Yes? You are sure?'

'It must have been so; I certainly carried their traps on board.'

'Now, are you quite positive it was the two o'clock going that way, and not the quarter past two returning from Geneva?' I had my Bradshaw handy, and was following the timetable with my fingers.

'The 2.15?' The gleam of light went out entirely from his stolid face. 'I have an idea you are right, sir. You see the two boats come in so near each other and lie at the same pier. I could easily make a mistake between them.'

'It is my firm belief,' I said, utterly disgusted with the fellow, 'my firm belief that you have made a mistake all through. You never saw the ladies at all, either of you.' I turned upon the conductor with a fierce scowl. 'You are a rank humbug; you have taken my money under false pretences. I've a precious good mind to report you to your superiors, and insist upon your refunding the money. You've swindled me out of it, thief and liar that you are.'

'Come, come, don't speak so freely. My superiors will always listen first to one of their own employees, and it will be awkward if I charge you with obstructing an official and making false charges against him.'

Mine is a hasty temper; I am constrained to confess to a fault which often stood in my way especially in my particular business. The conductor's insolence irritated me beyond measure, and coming as it did on the top of bitter disappointment I was driven into a deplorable access of rage, which I shall always regret. Without another word I rushed at him, caught him by the throat, and shook him violently, throwing him to the ground and beating his head upon it savagely.

Help must have come to him very speedily and to good purpose, for I soon found myself in custody, two colossal gendarmes holding me tight on each side. I was quickly removed like any malefactor to the lock-up in the town above, and was thus for the moment effectively precluded from continuing my pursuit.

Law and order are not to be lightly trifled with in Switzerland, least of all in the Canton de Vaud. I had been taken in the very act of committing a savage assault upon an official in the execution of his duty, which is true to the extent that every Swiss official conceives it to be his duty to outrage the feelings and tyrannize over inoffensive strangers.

The police of Lausanne showed me little consideration. I was not permitted to answer the charge against me, but was at once consigned to a cell, having been first searched and despoiled of all my possessions. Among them was my knife and a pocket revolver I generally carried, also my purse, my wallet with all my private papers, and my handbag. Both wallet and handbag were locked; they demanded the keys, thinking I had them hidden on my person, but I said they could find them for themselves, the truth being the locks were on a patent plan and could be opened with the fingers by any one who knew. This secret I chose to retain.

When alone in my gloomy prison, with leisure to reflect more calmly on my painful position, I realized what an ass I had been, and I vented my wrath chiefly on myself. But it was idle to repine. My object now was to go free again at the earliest possible moment, and I cast about to see how I might best compass it.

At first I was very humble, very apologetic. I acknowledged my error, and promised to do anything in my power to indemnify my victim. I offered him any money in reason, I would pay any sum they might fix, pay down on the nail and give my bond for the rest.

My gaolers scouted the proposal indignantly. Did I think justice was to be bought in Switzerland? It was the law I had outraged, not an individual merely. Besides — money is all powerful in this venal country — how could I pay, a poor devil like me, the necessary price? what could I produce in cash on the nail? My bond would not be worth the paper it was written on.

No, no, there was no chance for me; nothing could save me. I must go before the correctional police and pay in person for my offence. I might expect to be punished summarily, to be sent to gaol, to be laid by the heels for a month or two, perhaps more. Such a brutal assault as mine would be avenged handsomely.

Now I changed my tactics. I began to bluster. I was a British subject and claimed to be treated with proper respect. I appealed to the British Consul; I insisted upon seeing him. When they laughed at me, saying that he would not interfere with the course of justice on behalf of such an unknown vagabond, I told them roundly that I was travelling under the special protection of the British Minister for Foreign Affairs, the illustrious Marquis of Lansdowne. Let them bring me my wallet. I would show them my passport bearing the Royal Arms and the signature of one of H.M. Secretaries of State. All of us in the employ of Messrs. Becke invariably carried Foreign Office passports as the best credentials we could produce if we were caught in any tight place.

The greeting of so great a personage to his

trusty and well beloved Ludovic Tiler had a very marked effect upon my captors. It was enhanced by the sight of a parcel of crisp Bank of England notes lying snugly in the pocket of the wallet, which I had opened, but without betraying the secret of the spring. When I extracted a couple of fivers and handed them to the chief gaoler, begging him to do the best for my comfort, the situation changed considerably, but no hopes were held out for my immediate release. I was promised dinner from a restaurant hard by, and was permitted to send a brief telegram to Falfani, to the effect that I was detained at Lausanne by unforeseen circumstances, but no more. Then bedding was brought in, on which, after a night in the train, I managed to sleep soundly enough until quite late next morning.

I had summoned Eugène Falloon to my assistance, and he was permitted to visit me quite early, soon after the prison had opened. He was prompt and practical, and proceeded to perform the commissions I gave him with all despatch. I charged him first to telegraph to England, to our office, briefly stating my quandary, begging them to commend me to some one in Lausanne or Geneva, for Becke's have friends and correspondents in every city of the world. He was then to call upon the

British Consul, producing my passport in proof of my claim upon him as a British subject in distress, and if necessary secure me legal advice. I had been warned that I might expect to be examined that very day, but that several were likely to elapse before the final disposal of my case.

All that forenoon, and quite late into the next day, I was left brooding and chafing at my misfortune, self-inflicted I will confess, but not the less irksome to bear. I had almost persuaded myself that I should be left to languish here quite friendless and forgotten, when the luck turned suddenly, and daylight broke in to disperse my gloomy forebodings. Several visitors came, claiming to see me, and were presently admitted in turn. First came the Consul, and with him an intelligent Swiss advocate, who declared he would soon put matters right. It would only be a question of a fine, and binding me over to good behaviour on bail. Could I find bail? That was the only question. And while we still discussed it we found amongst the callers a respectable and well-to-do watchmaker from Geneva, who had been entreated (no doubt from Becke's) to do all that was needful on my behalf. I might be of good cheer; there was no reasonable doubt but that I should be released, but hardly before next day.

A second night in durance was not much to my taste, but I bore it with as much resignation as I could command; and when next morning I appeared before the Court, I paid my fine of one hundred francs with hearty good-will. I assured my bail, the friendly watchmaker, that he need not have the smallest fear I should again commit myself.

13

My spirits rose with my release, but there was still more than freedom to encourage my light-heartedness. I heard now and definitely of my fugitive lady. Falloon had come upon undoubted evidence that she had never left the great Jura-Simplon station, but had remained quietly out of sight in the 'ladies' waiting-room' until the next train left for Geneva. This was at 1.35 p.m., and she must have slipped away right under my eyes into the very train which had brought me back from Vevey. So near are the chances encountered in such a profession as ours.

Falloon had only ascertained this positively on the second day of my detention, but with it the information that only two first-class tickets, both for Geneva, had been issued by that train. To make it all sure he had taken the precaution to ask at all the stations along the line at which the train had stopped, seven in number, and had learned that no persons answering to my ladies had alighted at any of them. So my search was carried now to Geneva, and it might be possible to come upon my people there, although I was not oversanguine. I knew something of the place. I had been there more than once, had stayed some time, and I knew too well that it is a city with many issues, many facilities for travelling, and, as they had so much reason for moving on rapidly, the chances were that they would have already escaped me.

However, with Falloon I proceeded to Geneva without delay, and began a systematic search. We made exhaustive inquiries at the Cornavin station, where we arrived from Lausanne, and heard something.

The party had certainly been seen at this very station. Two ladies, one tall, the other short, with a baby. They had gone no further then; they had not returned to the station since. So far good. But there was a second station, the Gare des Vollondes, at the opposite end of the city, from which ran the short line to Bouveret on the south shore of the lake, and I sent Falloon there to inquire, giving him a rendezvous an hour later at the Café de la Couronne on the Quai du Lac. Meanwhile I meant to take all the hotels in regular order, and began with those of the first class on the right bank, the Beau Rivage, the Russie, de la Paix, National, Des Bergues, and the rest. As I drew blank everywhere I proceeded to try the hotels on the left bank, and made for the Pont de Mont Blanc to cross the Rhone, pointing for the Metropole.

Now my luck again greatly favoured me. Just as I put my foot upon the bridge I saw a figure approaching me, coming from the opposite direction.

I recognized it instantly. It was the lady herself.

She must have seen me at the very same moment, for she halted dead with the abruptness of one faced with a sudden danger, an opened precipice, or a venomous snake under foot. She looked hurriedly to right and left, as if seeking some loophole of escape.

At that moment one of the many electric trams that overspread Geneva with a network of lines came swinging down the Rue de Mont Blanc from the Cornavin station, and slackened speed at the end of the bridge. My lady made up her mind then and there, and as it paused she boarded it with one quick, agile spring.

With no less prompt decision I followed her, and we entered the car almost simultaneously.

There were only two seats vacant and, curiously enough, face to face. I took my place, not ill pleased, for she had already seen me, and I was anxious to know how my sudden reappearance would affect her. It was clear she did not relish it, or she would not have turned tail at our unexpected meeting.

I had not long to wait. She chose her line at once, and without hesitation addressed me, smiling and unabashed. Her self-possession, I had almost said her effrontery, took me quite aback.

'Surely I am not mistaken?' she began quite coolly. 'Have I not to thank you for your courtesy in the train a couple of days ago?'

I stammered a halting affirmative.

'I am afraid you must have thought me very rude. I ran off without a word, didn't I? The truth was my child had been suddenly taken ill and the nurse had to leave the train hurriedly. She had only just time to catch me and prevent me from going on. I am sorry. I should have liked to say good-bye.'

'Make no apologies, I beg,' I hastened to say courteously. But in my heart I trembled. What could this mean? Some fresh trick? She was so desperately full of guile!

'But I thought you were bound for the other end of the lake,' she continued. 'Do you make a long stay at Geneva?'

'No. Do you?' I retorted.

'Probably. I begin to like the place, and I have found very comfortable quarters at the Hôtel Cornavin, near the station. You may know it.'

Could this be really so? Her perfect frankness amazed me. I could not credit it, much less understand it. There was surely some pitfall, some trap concealed for my abounding credulity.

'I also propose to stay some days, but am not yet established.' I made so bold as to suggest that I had a great mind to try her Hôtel Cornavin.

'Why not?' she replied heartily. 'The accommodation is good, nice rooms, civil people, decent *cuisine*. It might suit you.'

She could not possibly have been more civil and gracious. Too civil by half, a more cautious man might have told himself.

The tram-car by this time had run through the Place Molard, the Allemand Marché, and was turning into the Rue de la Corraterie, pointing upward for the theatre and the Promenade des Bastions. Where was my involuntary companion bound?

She settled the question by getting out at the Place Neuve with a few parting words.

'I have a call to make near here. I had forgotten it. Perhaps I may hope to see you again. Do try the Cornavin. If so, *sans adieu*.'

Was it good enough? I could not allow her to slip through my fingers like this. What if her whole story was untrue, what if there was no Hôtel Cornavin, and no such guests there?

I could not afford to let her out of my sight, and with one spring I also left the car and, catching a last glimpse of her retreating skirts, gave chase.

I cannot say whether she realized that I was following, but she led me a pretty dance. In and out, and round and round, by narrow streets and dark passages, backwards and forwards, as adroitly as any practised thief eluding the hot pursuit of the police. At last she paused and looked back, and thinking she had shaken me off (for knowing the game well I had hastily effaced myself in a doorway) plunged into the entrance of a small unpretending hotel in a quiet, retired square — the Hôtel Pierre Fatio, certainly not the Cornavin.

The door in which I had taken shelter was that of a dark third-rate café well suited to my purpose, and well placed, for I was in full view of the Hôtel Pierre Fatio, which I was resolved to watch at least until my lady came out again. As I slowly absorbed an absinthe, revolving events past and to come, I thought it would be well to draw Falloon to me. It was past the hour for our meeting.

I scribbled three lines of a note and despatched it to the Café de la Couronne by a messenger to whom I fully described my colleague's appearance, desiring him to show the addressed envelope before delivery, but having no doubt that it would reach its destination.

Presently Falloon joined me, and as my lady had as yet made no sign, I bade him continue the watch, while I left the café openly and ostentatiously, so that it might be seen by any one curious to know that I had given up the game.

Far from it. I designed only to try the Hôtel Cornavin to ascertain the real facts; and if, as I shrewdly suspected, I had been fooled, to return forthwith and rejoin Falloon at the true point of interest, taking such further steps as might seem desirable. I was chiefly anxious to regain touch and combine forces with Falfani.

There was no mistake, however, at the Cornavin Hôtel. I had not been fooled. I was told directly I asked at the bureau that a Mrs. Blair, accompanied by her maid and child, was staying in the house. Could I see her? If monsieur would send up his card, it should be given her on her return. She was not at home for the moment. (I knew that.) Would monsieur call again?

I was slow to congratulate myself on what seemed a point gained, for I had still my misgivings, but I would make the most of the chances that offered to my hand. I secured a room at the Cornavin Hôtel, and bespoke another for Falfani, whom I should now summon at once. With this idea I took the earliest opportunity of telegraphing to him as follows:

'Detained by unfortunate *contretemps* at Lausanne, happily surmounted, clue lost and regained. Desire your cooperation. Come instantly, Hôtel Cornavin. She is here.

'Ludovic.'

I noted the time of despatch, 4.17 p.m. It would surely reach Falfani before the last train left Brieg coming my way, and I hardly trusted myself to anticipate the comfort and relief his appearance would bring me. Combined we could tie ourselves to our quarry, and never let her out of sight until our principals could take over and settle the business.

Then hailing a cab, I drove to a point close by where I had left Falloon, and found the situation entirely unchanged. No one had come out of the Hôtel Pierre Fatio. Mrs. Blair was paying a very long call, and I could not understand it. All the time I was haunted with a vague and ever present idea that she meant to sell me. The more I tortured my brain to consider how, the less I was able to fathom her intentions.

The time ran on, and I thought it would be

prudent to return to my own hotel. Mrs. Blair might have given us the slip, might have left by some other issue, and I felt that my place was at the Cornavin, where at least I knew she was staying. Falloon should stand his ground where he was, but I fully impressed upon him the importance of the duty entrusted to him.

I blessed my stars that I so decided. Mrs. Blair had not returned when the *table d'hôte* bell rang at the Cornavin, but I had hardly swallowed the first spoonful of soup when Falloon appeared, hot and flurried, with very startling news.

'*Elle se sauve*. She is saving herself; she is running away,' he cried. 'Already her carriage enters the station — without doubt she seeks the train for somewhere.'

I jumped up, rushed from the room, caught up my hat, and hurried across the Square of Place Cornavin into the station. It was a clear case of bolt. There she was ahead of me, quite unmistakable, walking quickly, with her fine upright figure clad in the same pearl grey ulster she had worn in the tram-car. She passed through the open doors of the waiting-room on to the platform where the train was waiting with engine attached.

'The 7.35 for Culoz and beyond by Amberieu to Paris,' I was informed on inquiry.

111

'A double back,' I concluded on the spot. She had had enough of it, and was going home again. In another minute or two she would have eluded me once more.

My only chance now lay in prompt action. I, too, must travel by this train. To secure a ticket and board it was soon done. I chose a carriage at no great distance from that she had entered; a through carriage to Mâcon, and which I was resolved to watch closely, but yet I did not mean to show myself to its occupants if it could be helped.

As we were on the point of starting, I scribbled a few lines on a leaf torn from my pocket-book to inform Falfani of my hasty departure and the reason for it. This I folded carefully and addressed to him, entrusting it to Falloon, who was to seek out my colleague at the Hôtel Cornavin after the arrival of the late train from Brieg, and deliver it. At the same time I handed Falloon a substantial fee, but desired him to offer his services to Falfani.

I saw no more of the lady. She did not show at Bellegarde when the French Customs' examination took place, nor yet at Culoz, and I believed she was now committed to the journey northward. But as I was dozing in my place and the train slowed on entering Amberieu, the guard whom I had suborned came to me with a hurried call.

'Monsieur, monsieur, you must be quick. Madame has descended and is just leaving the station. No doubt for the Hôtel de France, just opposite.'

There she was indeed with all her belongings. (How well I knew them by this time!) The maid with her child in arms, the porter with the light baggage.

I quickened my pace and entered the hotel almost simultaneously with her. Ranging up alongside I said, not without exultation:

'Geneva was not so much to your taste, then? You have left rather abruptly.'

'To whom are you speaking, sir?' she replied in a stiff, strange voice, assumed, I felt sure, for the occasion. She was so closely veiled that I could not see her face, but it was the same figure, the same costume, the same air. Lady Blackadder that was, Mrs. Blair as she now chose to call herself, I could have sworn to her among a thousand.

'It won't do, madame,' I insisted. 'I'm not to be put off. I know all about it, and I've got you tight, and I'm not going to leave go again. No fear.' I meant to spend the night on guard, watching and waiting till I was relieved by the arrival of the others, to whom I telegraphed without delay.

14

Colonel Annesley resumes

I left my narrative at the moment when I had promised my help to the lady I found in such distress in the Engadine express. I promised it unconditionally, and although there were circumstances in her case to engender suspicion, I resolutely ignored them. It was her secret, and I was bound to respect it, content to await the explanation I felt sure she could make when so minded.

It was at dinner in the dining-car, under the eyes of her persecutor, that we arranged to give him the slip at Basle. It was cleverly accomplished, I think.

(Here the Colonel gives an account of all that happened between Basle and Brieg; and as the incidents have been already described by Falfani it is unnecessary to retell them, except to note that Annesley had quickly discovered the detective's escape outside Goeschenen and lost no time in giving chase.)

As may be supposed I rejoiced greatly on reaching Brieg to find that Falfani had been bitterly disappointed. It was plain from the telegram that was handed to him on arrival, and which so upset him that he suffered me to take it out of his hand and to read it for myself, that a friend, his colleague, no doubt, had been checked summarily at Lausanne. He said he had lost 'her,' the lady of course.

I was not altogether happy in my mind about her, for when we had parted at Brieg it had been settled that she should take the Simplon route through this very place Brieg, at which I now found myself so unexpectedly, and I ought to have come upon her or had news of her somewhere had her plans been carried out. She certainly had not reached Brieg, for with my ally l'Echelle we searched the town for news of her that night and again next morning.

The situation was embarrassing. I could decide upon no clear course but that of holding on to Falfani and clinging to him with the very skin of my teeth; any light must come from or through him, or at least by keeping him in full view I might prevent him from doing any more mischief.

One of us, l'Echelle or myself, continually watched him all that day, the third of this curious imbroglio into which I was plunged. At night I took the strong and unjustifiable measure of locking him into his room.

When he discovered it next morning he was furious, and came straight at me open-mouthed.

'I'll appeal to the law, I'll denounce you to the authorities, I'll charge you with persecution and with false imprisonment. You shall be arrested. I'll be rid of you somehow, you shall not stay here, you shall leave Brieg.'

'With all my heart — when you do. Have I not told you that already? Where you go I go, where you stay I stay.'

'But it is most monstrous and abominable. I will not submit to it. You have no sort of right to act in this way. Why is it?'

'You can guess my reasons, surely. Only it is not for your *beaux yeux*; not because I like you. I loathe and detest you. You are a low, slimy spy, who richly deserves to be thrashed for bullying a lady.'

'I'll have you to know, sir, that I am fully entitled to act as I am doing,' he said with a consequential air. 'I am the representative of a court of law; I have great people at my back, people who will soon bring you to book. Wait a little, we shall see. You'll sing a very poor song when you have to do with a nobleman. The Right Honourable the Earl of Blackadder will arrive shortly. I hope this very afternoon. You can settle it with him, ah! How do you like that, eh?'

I laughed him to scorn.

'Psha, man, you're an ass. I've told you before now what I think of Lord Blackadder, and if it be necessary I'll tell him to his face when he gets here.'

This conversation took place just before the *table-d'hôte* luncheon, and immediately afterwards Falfani went out in the direction of the railway station. I followed, keeping him in sight on the platform, where, by and by, I saw him, hat in hand, bowing obsequiously before a passenger who alighted from the incoming train. It would have been enough for me had I not already known Lord Blackadder by sight. They walked back together to the hotel, and so, at a certain distance, did I.

I was lounging about outside the house, wondering what would happen next, when a waiter came out to me bearing a card, which he tendered, bowing low, more in deference to the card, as I thought, than to me.

'Earl of Blackadder' was the name engraved, and written just below in pencil were the words, 'would like to speak to Colonel Annesley at once.'

'Well, I've no objection,' I began, stiffly. I thought the summons a trifle too peremptory. 'Where is he?'

The waiter pointed back to the hotel, and I saw a white, evil face glowering at me from a

117

window on the ground floor of the hotel. The very look on it stirred my bile. It was an assumption of superiority, of concentrated pride and exaggerated authority, as though everyone must yield to his lightest wish and humble himself in the dust before him. I resented this, and slipping the card carelessly in my pocket, I nodded to the waiter, who still stood awaiting my reply.

'Will monsieur come?' he asked.

'No. Tell his lordship he will find me here if he wants me. That will do,' and I waved him off.

Soon afterwards Lord Blackadder came out. Mahomet came to the mountain. I liked his face less than ever. It wore an angry scowl now; his dark eyes glittered balefully under the close-knit eyebrows, his lips were drawn down, and the curved nose was like the aggressive beak of a bird of prey.

'Colonel Annesley, I understand,' he said coldly, contemptuously, just lifting one finger towards the brim of his hat.

'That is my name,' I responded, without returning the salute.

'I am Lord Blackadder; you will have had my card. I desired to address you somewhat more privately than this.' He looked round the open yard in front of the hotel. 'May I hope you will accompany me to my rooms? I have to speak to you on a matter that concerns you very closely.'

'That I cannot admit. There can be nothing between you and me, Lord Blackadder, that concerns me very closely; nothing that the whole world may not hear.'

'What I have to say might prove very unpleasant to you in the telling, Colonel Annesley. You would be well advised in agreeing that our interview should be private.'

'I can't see it, and I must tell you plainly that I do not care one jot. Say what you please, my lord, and, if you like, as loud as you please, only be quick about it.'

'With all my heart, then, if you will have it so. I wish to tell you, Colonel Annesley, that you have taken a most unwarrantable liberty in mixing yourself up with my affairs.'

'I am not aware that I have done so.'

'You shall not trifle with me, sir. Your conduct is inexcusable, ungentlemanlike.'

'Take care, my lord,' I broke in hotly.

'People who forget themselves so far as you have done must accept the responsibility of their own actions; and I tell you, here and now, that I shall call you to strict account for yours.'

The man was trying me hard, but still I strove to keep my temper.

'I don't care that for your opinion, and I do

119

not allow that you are a judge of what is gentlemanlike. No one would do so who had read the public prints lately.'

'How dare you, sir, refer to my conduct, or presume to criticize or question it?' he burst out.

'Ta, ta, ta! It is a real pleasure to me to tell you what I think of you, Lord Blackadder; and as I am ready to give you every satisfaction, I shall not stint myself.'

'I insist upon satisfaction.'

'By all means. It can be easily arranged. We are within a short step of either France or Italy, and in both countries the old-fashioned plan of settling affairs of honour is still in force. We shall find friendly seconds in the nearest garrison town, and I shall be glad to cross the frontier with you whenever you please.'

'You talk like the hectoring, swashbuckling bully that you are,' he cried angrily, but looking rather uncomfortable . . . 'I will swear the peace against you.'

'Do so by all means. It would be like you. A man who would descend to espionage, who could so cruelly misuse a lady, is capable of anything; of making assertions he cannot substantiate, of threatening things he dare not do.'

'I have the clearest proof of what I say. You

have chosen to come into my life — '

'I should be extremely sorry to do so.'

'Will you deny that you have sided with my enemies, that you have joined and abetted them in a base plot to defraud and rob me of my — my — property, of that which I most highly value and cherish of all my possessions?'

'I don't know what you are talking about, Lord Blackadder, but whatever your grievance I tell you candidly that I do not like your tone or your manner, and I shall hold no further converse with you.'

I turned my back on him and walked away.

'Stay, stay. You must and shall hear me out. I've not done with you.' He came hurrying after me, following close and raising his voice higher and higher. 'Your very presence here is an offence. You have no right to be here at all.'

'Do you think that you own all Switzerland, my noble earl?' I answered over my shoulder as I walked on. 'It is not your ground to warn me off.'

'I tell you you shall not remain here to annoy me and work against me. I forbid it, and I will put a stop to it. I give you plain warning.'

'You know you are talking nonsense. I shall go my own road, and I defy you to do your worst.'

Here, when I was on the threshold of the hotel, I met Falfani full, as he came running out excitedly, holding in his hand the telltale blue envelope, which, with his elated air, indicated clearly that he had just received important news.

I paused for a moment, hoping he might commit himself, and was rewarded by hearing him say aloud:

'It is from Geneva, my lord, from Ludovic Tiler,' he began indiscreetly, and was angrily silenced by my lord, who called him 'a triple-dyed idiot,' and with a significant gesture towards me bade him walk away to some distance from the hotel.

The mischief was done, however, for I had of course heard enough to know that the other detective had given signs of life at last, and that the report, to judge by Falfani's glee, must be satisfactory. The more pleased the other side, the more reason to fear that matters were adverse on ours.

15

It might be thought that I was too hard on my Lord Blackadder, but only those few indeed who were unacquainted with the circumstances of his divorce would find fault with me. The scandal was quite recent, and the Blackadder case had been in everybody's mouth. The papers had been full of it, and the proceedings were not altogether to his lordship's credit. They had been instituted by him, however, on grounds that induced the jury to give him a verdict, and the judge had pronounced a decree nisi on the evidence as it stood.

Yet the public sympathies were generally with the respondent, the Countess of Blackadder. It had been an unhappy marriage, an ill-assorted match, mercenary, of mere convenience, forced upon an innocent and rather weak girl by careless and callous guardians, eager to rid themselves of responsibility for the two twin sisters, Ladies Claire and Henriette Standish, orphans, and with no near relations.

Lord Blackadder was immensely rich, but a man of indifferent moral character, a *roué* and a voluptuary, with a debilitated constitution and an unattractive person, possessing none of the gifts that take a maiden's fancy.

Estrangement soon followed the birth of the son and heir to his title and great estates. My lord was a great deal older than his beautiful young wife, and desperately jealous of her. Distrust grew into strong suspicion, and presently consumed him when an old flame of Lady Henriette's, Charlie Forrester, of the Dark Horse, turned up from foreign service, and their names came to be bracketed together by the senseless gossiping busybodies ever ready to tear a pretty woman's reputation to tatters. It was so much put about, so constantly dinned into Lord Blackadder's ears, that he was goaded into a perfect fury, and was at length determined, by hook or by crook, to put away his wife, leaving it to certain astute and well-practised solicitors to manufacture a clear, solid case against her.

Lady Blackadder, who hated and despised her lord, foolishly played into his hands. She never really went wrong, so her friends stoutly averred, especially her sister Claire, a staunch and loyal soul, but she gave a handle to innuendo, and more than once allowed appearances to go against her.

There was one very awkward story that

could not be disproved as it was told, and in the upshot convicted her. It was clearly shown in evidence that she had made up her mind to leave Lord Blackadder; more, that she meant to elope with Major Forrester. It was said, but not so positively, that she had met him at Victoria Station; they were seen there together, had travelled by the same train, and there was a strong presumption that they had arrived together at Brighton; one or two railway officials deposed to the fact.

Lady Blackadder denied this entirely, and gave a very different complexion to the story. She had gone to Brighton; yes, but quite alone. Major Forrester had seen her off, no doubt, but they had parted at the carriage door. Her visit to Brighton had been for the purpose of seeing and staying with an old servant, once a very confidential maid for whom she had a great liking, and had often taken refuge with when worried and in trouble. She thought, perhaps, to make this the first stage in the rupture with my lord.

This maid had earnestly adjured her not to break with her husband, and to return to Grosvenor Square.

This flight was the head and corner-stone of Lady Blackadder's offending. It was interpreted into guilt of the most heinous kind; the evidence in support of it seemed overwhelming. Witnesses swore positively to the companionship of Major Forrester, both at Victoria and Brighton, and it was to be fairly assumed that they were at the latter place together.

No rebutting evidence was forthcoming. The maid, a woman married to an ex-French or Swiss courier, by name Bruel, could not be produced, simply because she could not be found in Brighton. They were supposed to be settled there as lodging-house keepers, but they had not resided long enough to be in the Directory, and their address was not known. Lord Blackadder's case was that they were pure myths, they had never had any tangible existence, but were only imported into the case to support an ingenious but untenable defence.

It was more than hinted that they had been spirited away, and they were not the first material witnesses, it was hinted, in an intricate case, conducted by Messrs. Gadecker and Gobye, who had mysteriously disappeared. So the plausible, nay, completely satisfactory explanation of Lady Blackadder's visit to Brighton could not be put forward, much less established, and there was no sort of hope for her. She lost her case in the absence of the Bruels, man and wife. The verdict was for Lord Blackadder, and he was adjudged to have the care and custody of the child, the infant Viscount Aspdale.

I had not the smallest doubt when I realized with whom I had to do that the unhappy mother had made a desperate effort to redress her wrongs, as she thought them, and had somehow contrived to carry off her baby before she could be deprived of it.

I had met her in full flight upon the Engadine express.

What next? Was she to be overtaken and despoiled, legally, of course, but still cruelly, separated from her own flesh and blood? The Court might order such an unnatural proceeding, but I was moved by every chivalrous impulse to give her my unstinting and unhesitating support to counteract it.

I was full of these thoughts, and still firmly resolved to help Lady Blackadder, when l'Echelle, the conductor whose services I still retained, sought me out hurriedly, and told me that he believed the others were on the point of leaving Brieg.

'I saw Falfani and milord poring over the pages of the *Indicateur*, and heard the word Geneva dropped in a whisper. I think they mean to take the next train along the lake shore.'

'Not a doubt of it,' I assented; 'so will we. They must not be allowed to go beyond our reach.'

When the 6.57 p.m. for Geneva was due out from Brieg, we, l'Echelle and I, appeared on the platform, and our intention to travel by it was made plain to Lord Blackadder. The effect upon him was painfully manifest at once. He chafed, he raged up and down, grimacing and apostrophizing Falfani; once or twice he approached me with clenched fists, and I really thought would have struck me at last. Seeing me enter the same carriage with him, with the obvious intention of keeping him under my eye, he threw himself back among the cushions and yielded himself with the worst grace to the inevitable.

The railway journey was horribly slow, and it must have been past 11 p.m. before we reached Geneva. We alighted in the Cornavin station, and as they moved at once towards the exit I followed. I expected them to take a carriage and drive off, and was prepared to give chase, when I found they started on foot, evidently to some destination close at hand. It proved to be the Cornavin Hôtel, not a stone's-throw from the station.

They entered, and went straight to the bureau, where the night clerk was at his desk. I heard them ask for a person named Tiler, and without consulting his books the clerk replied angrily:

'Tiler! Tiler! *Ma foi*, he is of no account,

your Tiler. He has gone off from the dinner-table and without paying his bill.'

'That shall be made all right,' replied Lord Blackadder loftily, as he detailed his name and quality, before which the employee bowed low. 'And might I ask,' his lordship went on, 'whether a certain Mrs. Blair, a lady with her child and its nurse, is staying in the hotel?'

'But certainly, milord. They have been here some days. Salon and suite No. 17.'

'At any rate, that's well, Falfani,' said Lord Blackadder, with a sigh of satisfaction. 'But what of your friend Tiler? Thick-headed dolt, unable to keep awake, I suppose.'

At that moment a shabbily dressed person approached Falfani, touched his hat, and offered him a note, saying:

'This must be for you, monsieur. I heard your name — '

'From Tiler, my lord, aha! This explains.' And he passed the scrap of paper on to his employer.

'I'll be hanged if I see it! He says the parties have gone, and that he is in close attendance; yet this fellow here,' pointing to the clerk, 'assures us she is in this very house. I don't understand it, by Gad!'

'There is some fresh trick, my lord, you may be sure. The devil himself isn't half so clever as this fine lady. But we'll get at the bottom of it. We shall hear more from Tiler, and we've got the lady here, under our hand.'

'Ah! but have we? This chap's as likely as not to be mistaken. How do you know, sir,' to the clerk, 'that Mrs. Blair is still in the hotel? When did you come on duty? What if she left without your knowing it?'

'It could not be, milord. See, it is marked in the register. No. 17 is occupied. I could not let it. Mrs. Blair holds it still.'

'But she may not be in it, all the same. Can't you see? She may retain it, but not use it.'

'Look, my lord, look, there's one of her party, anyway,' interposed Falfani, and he called his attention to a female figure standing a little aloof in the shadow of the staircase, and which I had already recognized.

It was Philpotts, 'Mrs. Blair's' maid, and she was trying to attract my attention. Lord Blackadder had not seen her, and now his eye, for the first time, fell upon me. He turned on me furiously.

'You! You! Still at my heels? This is perfectly monstrous. It amounts to persecution. You still dare to intrude yourself. Can I have no privacy? Take yourself off, or I will not answer for the consequences.'

I confess I only laughed and still held my

ground, although my lord's outcry had attracted much attention. Several people ran up, and they might have sided against me, when I heard a voice whisper into my ear:

'Come, sir, come. Slip away. My lady is dying to see you. She is terribly upset.'

16

I was received with great warmth and cordiality by my friend, and it was made clear to me that my opportune appearance brought her great comfort and support.

'I never hoped for such good fortune as this,' she began heartily. 'I had no idea you were within miles, and was repining bitterly that I had let you get so far out of the way. Now you appear in the very nick of time, just when I was almost in despair. But wait. Can I still count upon your help?'

'Why, most certainly, Lady Blackadder.'

'Lady Black — ' She was looking at me very keenly, and, as I thought, was much startled and surprised. Then with a conscious blush she went on. 'Of course, I might have guessed you would penetrate my disguise, but you must not call me Lady Blackadder. I can lay no claim to the title.'

'May I be forgiven if I trench on such a delicate subject, and assure you of my most sincere sympathy? Everybody felt for you deeply. I hope you will believe that I am, and ever shall be, at your orders and devoted to your service.'

'Yes, yes, I am sure of it; I know I can depend upon you fully, and I mean to do so now at once. You know, you have heard, that Lord Blackadder is here, and actually in this hotel?'

'I came with him. I was watching that fellow, the detective Falfani, when his lordship came upon the scene. We had words, a quarrel, almost a fight.'

'Pfu! He would not fight! I only wish you had thrashed him as he deserves. But that won't help matters now. How am I to escape him?'

'With the child?'

'To be sure. Of course, I do not fear him in the least for myself.'

'You want to keep the child?'

'Naturally, as I carried it off.'

'And still more because you had the best right to it, whatever the Court might direct. You are its mother.'

Again she blushed and smiled, rather comically. 'I certainly shall not surrender it to Lord Blackadder, not without a struggle. Yet he is very near getting it now.'

'In there?' I nodded towards the next room. 'It is a close thing. How are you to manage it?'

'There would not have been the slightest difficulty; it was all but done, and then some

133

one, something, failed me. I expected too much perhaps, but I have been bitterly disappointed, and the danger has revived.'

'Come, come, Lady Blackadder, keep up your courage. Let us take counsel together. We can surely devise some fresh plan. Don't give way now; you have been so plucky all through. Be brave still.'

'Thank you, Colonel Annesley, I will.' She put out her hand with enchanting frankness, her fine eyes shining gratefully. A man would have dared much, endured much, to win such gracious approval.

'It is getting late, but you must hear all I have to tell before we can decide upon the next step. Will you listen to me? I shall not bore you. It is a long story. First let me clear the ground a little. I must disabuse your mind on one point. I am not Lady Blackadder — no, no, do not misunderstand me — not on account of the divorce, but I never was Lady Blackadder. She was Henriette Standish. I am Claire, her sister Claire.'

'What a fool I've been!' I cried. 'I might have guessed.'

'How should you? But let me go on. I shall never forget that detestable trial, those awful days in the Divorce Court, when the lawyers fought and wrangled over my darling sister, like dogs over a bone, tearing and snarling at each other, while the judge sat above like a solemn old owl, never moving or making a sign.

'Henriette positively refused to appear in the case, although she was pressed and entreated by her legal advisers. She could have thrown so much light on the worst and darkest part. She could have repudiated the cowardly charges made, and cast back the lies drawn round her to ruin her. If the jury had but seen her pretty, pathetic face, and heard from her own sweet lips all she had endured, they would have come to a very different verdict.

'But she would not come forward on her own behalf. She would not defend the action; she did not want to win it, but waited till it was all over, hiding herself away in a far-off corner of the Apennines, where I was to join her with the child, little Ralph.

'There had been no question of that; the possibility of her losing it had never been raised, or she would have nerved herself to fight sooner than give up what she valued more than her very life.

'It fell upon me with crushing effect, although towards the end of the trial I had had my forebodings. Lord Blackadder was to have the custody of his heir, and my dear sweet Henriette was to be robbed for ever of her chiefest joy and treasure. The infant child was to be abandoned to strangers, paid by its unnatural and unfeeling father.

'I had braced myself to listen to all that came out in court, a whole tissue of lies told by perjured wretches whose evidence was accepted as gospel — one of them was the same Falfani whom you know, and who had acted the loathsome part of spy on several occasions.

'Directly the judge had issued his cruel fiat, I slipped out, hurried down-stairs into the Strand, jumped into a hansom, and was driven at top speed to Hamilton Terrace, bent upon giving instant effect to a scheme I had long since devised.

'I found my faithful Philpotts awaiting me with everything prepared as I had arranged. The dear baby was dressed quickly — he was as good as gold — the baggage, enough for my hurried journey to Fuentellato, had been packed for days past, and we took the road.

'I knew that pursuit would not tarry, but I was satisfied that I had made a good start, and I hoped to make my way through to Italy without interference. When I first saw you at Calais I was seized with a terrible fear, which was soon allayed; you did not look much like a detective, and you were already my good friend when the real ruffian, Falfani, came on board the train at Amiens.'

(Lady Claire Standish passed on next to describe her journey from Basle to Lausanne, and the clever way in which she eluded the second detective — matters on which the reader has been already informed.)

'On reaching Geneva I at once opened communications with Henriette. I felt satisfied, now that I had come so far, it would be well that she should join me, and that we should concert together as to our next proceedings. Our first and principal aim was to retain the child at all costs and against all comers. I had no precise knowledge as to where we should be beyond the jurisdiction of the English law, but I could not believe that the Divorce Court and its emissaries could interfere with us in a remote Italian village. My real fear was of Lord Blackadder. He was so bold and unscrupulous that, if the law would not help him, he would try stratagem, or even force. We should be really safe nowhere if we once came within his reach, and, the best plan to keep out of his clutches was to hide our whereabouts from him.

'Fuentellato would not do, for although I do not believe he knew the exact spot in which Henriette had taken refuge, he must have guessed something from the direction of my journey, and that I was on my way to join her. If he failed to intercept me *en route*, he would make his way straight there. I had resolved he should not find us, but where else should we go? Farther afield, if necessary to the very end of the world. Lord Blackadder, we might be sure, would hunt high and low to recover his lost heir, sparing no expense, neglecting no means.

'It was, however, essential to elude his agents, who were so near at hand and likely to press me close. That was another reason for drawing my sister to me. I had hit upon a cunning device, as I thought it, to confuse and deceive my pursuers, to throw them on to a false scent, lead them to follow a red herring, while the fox, free of the hunt, took another line.'

17

'There should be two Richmonds in the field! That was my grand idea. Two sets, two parties, each of them consisting of one lady, one maid, and one baby, exactly similar and indistinguishable. When the time was ripe we should separate, and each would travel in opposite directions, and I hoped to show sufficient guile to induce my persecutors to give chase to the wrong quarry. Run it to the death, while the party got clear away.

'I had made a nice calculation. Fuentellato was at no great distance from Parma, on the main line of railway. If she started at once, via Piacenza to Turin, she could catch the Mont Cenis express through to Modane and Culoz, where she could change for Geneva, so as to reach me some time on Tuesday.

'This was exactly what happened. My sister carried out my instructions to the letter, and I met her here on arrival. I had taken up my quarters in this hotel because it was so near the station, but I thought it prudent that Henriette should lodge somewhere else, the farther the better, and she went to a small place, the Hôtel Pierre Fatio, at the other end of the town.

'It is a long story, Colonel Annesley, but there is not much more, and yet the most interesting part is to come.

'We now devoted ourselves to the practical carrying out of the scheme, just we four women; our maids, both clever dressmakers, were of immense help. It was soon done. You can buy anything in Geneva. There are plenty of good shops and skilful workers, and we soon provided ourselves with the clothes, all the disguises really that we required — the long grey dust cloaks and soft hats and all the rest, so much alike that we might have been soldiers in the same regiment. Philpotts and Victorine, my sister's maid, were also made up on a similar pattern, and a second baby was built up as a dummy that would have deceived any one.

'Everything was completed by this morning, and I had settled that my sister, with her dear little Ralph, should get away, but by quite a new route, while I held my ground against the detectives. I felt sure they would soon hear of me and run me down. I hoped they would attach themselves to me, and meant to lead them a fine dance as a blind for Henriette, who, meanwhile, would have crossed to Lyons and gone south to

Marseilles. The Riviera is a longer and more roundabout road to Turin, but it was open, and I hoped unimpeded. What do you think of my diplomacy?'

'Admirable!' I cried, with enthusiasm. 'Your cleverness, Lady Claire, is colossal. Go on, I beg of you. Surely you have succeeded?'

'Alas! no. Everything was cut and dried and this evening we scored the first point in the game. Henriette went on this evening to Amberieu, the junction for Lyons. She went straight from her hotel, alone, for of course I was obliged to keep close, or the trick would have been discovered, and it was in part.

'For I must tell you that to-day one of the detectives appeared in Geneva, not the first man, but a second, who attached himself to me at Basle. I met him plump on the Mont Blanc Bridge and turned tail, but he came after me. I jumped into a passing tram, so did he, and to throw him off his guard I talked to him, and made friends with him, and advised him to come and stay at this hotel. Then I got out and left him, making my way to the Pierre Fatio Hôtel by a circuitous route, dodging in and out among the narrow streets till I nearly lost myself.

'I thought I had eluded him, and he certainly was nowhere near when I went into the hotel. But I suppose he followed me, he must have, and found out something, for I know now that he went to Amberieu after Henriette — '

'You are perfectly sure?'

'She has telegraphed to me from Amberieu; I got it not an hour ago. The man accosted her, taking her for me. He would have it she was Mrs. Blair, and told her to her face that he did not mean to lose sight of her again. So you see — '

'If she goes round by Lyons to Marseilles, then, he would be at her heels, and the scheme breaks down in that respect?'

'Not only that, I don't see that he could interfere with her, or do her much harm, and at Marseilles she might change her plans entirely. There are ever so many ways of escape from a seaport. She might take ship and embark on board the first steamer bound to the East, for India or Ceylon, the Antipodes or far Cathay.'

'Well, why not?'

'Henriette, my sister, has given way. Her courage has failed her at this, the most critical moment, when she is within a hair's breadth of success. She is afraid to go on alone with little Ralph, and is running back to me by the first train to-morrow morning, at five or six o'clock.'

'Coming here? Into the very mouths of all the others!'

'Just so, and all my great scheme will be ruined. They cannot but find out, and there is no knowing what they may do. Lord Blackadder, I know, is capable of anything. I assure you, Colonel Annesley, I am in despair. What *can* I do?'

She looked at me in piteous appeal, the tears brimming over, her hands stretched towards me with a gesture at once pathetic and enchanting.

'Say, rather, what can *we* do, Lady Claire,' I corrected her. 'This is my business, too, if you will allow me to say so, and I offer you my advice for what it is worth.'

'Yes, I will take it thankfully, I promise you.'

'The only safe course now is the boldest. You must make another exchange with your sister, Lady Blackadder — '

'Call her Lady Henriette Standish. She has dropped the other entirely.'

'By all means. Lady Henriette then has determined to take the first train from Amberieu at — Have you a Bradshaw? Thank you — at 5.52 a.m., which will get her to Culoz at 6.48. You must, if possible, exchange babies, and at the same time exchange *rôles*. I feel sure that you, at any rate, are not afraid of going to Marseilles with the real baby.'

'Hardly!' she laughed scornfully. 'But Henriette — what is to become of her?'

'That shall be my affair. It is secondary, really. The first and all-important is for you to secure the little Ralph and escape with him. It will have to be done under the very eyes of the enemy, for there is every reason to fear they will be going on, too. The other detective, this Tiler — I have heard them call him by that name — will have told them of her ladyship's movements, and will have summoned them, Falfani at least, to his side.'

'If I go on by that early train they will, no doubt, do the same. I must not be seen by them. They would fathom the trick of the two parties and the exchange.'

'Yet you must go on by that train. It's the only way.'

'Of course I might change my appearance a little, but not enough to deceive them. Cannot I go across to the station before them and hide in some compartment specially reserved for us?'

'It might be managed. We might secure the whole of the seats.'

'Money is no object.'

'It will do most things, especially in Switzerland. Leave it to me, Lady Claire. All you have to do is to be ready to-morrow morning, very early, remember. Before 5 a.m.'

'If necessary I'll sit up all night.'

'Well, then, that's settled. I'll knock at your door and see you get some coffee.'

'Philpotts shall make it; no one in the hotel must know. There will be the bill.'

'I will see to that. I'll come back after you're ensconced, with the blinds drawn. Sick lady on the way, via Culoz to Aix-les-Bains, must not be disturbed. It won't matter my being seen on the road, all the better really if my lord is there, for I have a little plan of my own, Lady Claire — no, please don't ask me yet — but it will help matters, I think.'

'You are, indeed, my true and faithful friend,' she said, as she put out her hand and wished me good night. She left it in mine for just a second, and I flattered myself that its warm pressure was meant to assure me that I had established a substantial claim to her regard.

18

On leaving Salon No. 17 I descended to the ground floor, seeking the smoking-room and a little stimulant to assist me in deciding the best course of action for the following day.

As I passed along the corridor I caught sight of l'Echelle, whom I considered my man, in close confabulation with Falfani in a quiet corner. They could hardly have seen me, at least l'Echelle made no reference to the fact when he came to me presently and asked if I had any orders for the morning. I answered him sternly:

'What was Falfani saying to you just now? The truth, please, or you get nothing more from me.'

'He is a *vaurien* and *fainéant*, and thinks others as bad as himself; said my lord would give me five hundred francs to know what you were doing, and find out whether the lady who travelled with us to Basle last Sunday is here in this house.'

'I've no objection to your taking his money if you will tell me something. How long does my lord mean to stay here? Have you any idea?'

'They all go on by the early train to Culoz or farther. A pressing telegram has come from their man at Amberieu.'

'Ah! Indeed. Then you may say that I am also going by that early train. They're not going to shake me off very easily. Tell them that, and that if they want the lady they'd better look for her. She isn't here.'

I lied in a good cause, for a lady, as a gentleman is bound to do. I shall be forgiven, I think, under the circumstances.

The free use of coin had the desired effect at the railway station. Soon after 5 a.m. I was met at a private door and escorted, with my precious party, by a circuitous route to where the 5.48 was shunted, waiting the moment to run back to the departure platform. There was a coupé ready for Lady Claire, and she took her place quietly, observed by no one but the obsequious official who had managed it all.

As for me, I walked boldly to the hotel and hung about the hall till the Blackadder party appeared and had left for the station. Then I asked the hotel clerk for Lady Claire's bill, paid it, with my own, and went over to the train, selecting a compartment close to the coupé. As I passed it I knocked lightly on the window pane, giving a signal previously arranged between us.

I do not think that Lord Blackadder saw me then, at the start. But at Bellegarde, the Swiss frontier, where there was a wait of half an hour for the Customs examination, an irritating performance always, but carried out here with the most maddening and overbearing particularity, everyone was obliged to alight from the train, and for the moment I trembled for Lady Claire. But the appeal addressed to the French brigadier, 'un galant homme,' of an invalid lady, too ill to be disturbed, was effectual, especially when backed by two five-franc pieces.

Lord Blackadder was on the platform with the rest, and directly he saw me he came up with the same arrogant air, curiously blended with aggrieved helplessness.

'This will end badly, Colonel Annesley. I give you fair warning. I shall appeal to the authorities. We shall be on French soil directly, and I know something of French law. It affords protection to all who claim it against such people as you.'

'If you talk like that I'll give you some reason to seek the protection of the gendarmes or police,' I cried, but checked myself at once.

I had made up my mind how to deal with him, but the time was not yet.

'Your insolence, sir, outsteps all bounds,

and you shall answer for it, I tell you.'

But now the cry was raised '*En voiture! en voiture!*' and we were peremptorily hustled back to our seats. Lord Blackadder hurried to his compartment at the end of the train some way from mine and the coupé. As I passed the latter, seeing the road clear, I gave the signal, and, taking out my railway carriage key, quickly slipped in.

She received me with her rare sweet smile, that was the richest payment a man could ask.

'The critical moment is at hand, Lady Claire,' I said, speaking mysteriously. 'It is essential that we should have a few last words together. Naturally we must now be guided very much by the way things happen, but so far as possible we must prepare for them. We have managed capitally so far. I don't believe Lord Blackadder has any idea you are in the train, and I much doubt that he expects to find Lady Henriette at Culoz. You think she will really be there?'

'I feel sure of it. It is just what she would do.'

'Then everything will depend on you. You must be alert and prompt, on the *qui vive* to seize your opportunity. It will be your business to make your way to her with the dummy the instant the train stops.'

'I shall have to find her.'

'That is the first and chief thing on your part. You *must* find her at once. There are very few minutes for the whole job. Find her, exchange burthens, send her to the train for Aix-les-Bains. It will be waiting there. You hurry back to this coupé, lie low, and, if all goes well, you will be travelling on toward Amberieu before the enemy has the least notion what has occurred.'

'But one word, please. What will the enemy have been doing at Culoz? Say they catch sight of Henriette as soon as we do?'

'I hope and trust they may. I count upon that as part of my programme.'

'But they will catch her, stop her, deprive her of our dear little Ralph.'

'Wait, wait. You will see. It will be settled in a moment now. But before it is too late let us arrange how you may communicate with me. We shall both be moving about, and the best address I can give will be in London. Telegraph to me there to my club, the Mars and Neptune, Piccadilly. I will send instructions there to have all telegrams opened and retelegraphed to me at once. They shall be kept informed of my whereabouts daily. But now, here we are, close to Culoz and already slowing down. Look out, please.'

It could not have suited me better. There,

standing under the shadow of the dwarf plane-trees, but with not the slightest suggestion of concealment, was the exact counterpart of Lady Claire, her twin sister, Lady Henriette Standish, till lately Lady Blackadder. She was staring intently at our train as it ran in, deeply anxious, no doubt, to note the arrival of her sister.

'Give me a short start,' I said to Lady Claire as I jumped out of the coupé. 'You will see why.'

Even as I spoke I was satisfied that the pursuing party had recognized the object of their journey. They had all alighted and were coming up the platform in great haste to where she stood. Had any doubt remained, it would have been removed by the appearance of a man who ran out from some back part of the station and waved them forward with much gesticulation.

Here I interposed, and, rushing forward with all the ardour of a football player entering a scrimmage, I took Lord Blackadder by the throat and shook him.

19

Falfani again

When that audacious and intemperate English
Colonel so far forgot himself as to assault my
lord the Right Honourable the Earl of Blackadder at Culoz Station in the open light of
day before us all, I greatly rejoiced; for, although
horror-stricken at his ruffianly conduct, I knew
that he would get his deserts at last. The
French authorities would certainly not toler-
ate brawling in the precincts of the railway
station, and justice must promptly overtake
the sole offender. The blackguard Colonel,
the cause and origin of the disturbance, would,
of course, be at once arrested and removed.

The fracas had naturally attracted general
attention. One or two porters ran up and
endeavoured, with Tiler and myself, to rescue
my lord from his cowardly assailant. A crowd
quickly gathered around us, many passengers
and a number of idlers, who drop from
nowhere, as it might be, all drawn to the spot
by overmastering curiosity. Everybody talked
at the same time, asking questions, volunteering answers, some laughing shamelessly at my

lord's discomfiture, a few expressing indignation, and declaring that such a scandal should not be permitted, and the guilty parties held strictly to account.

The gendarmes on duty — a couple of them are always at hand in a French railway station — soon appeared, and, taking in the situation at the first glance, imposed silence peremptorily.

'Let some one, one person only, speak and explain.' The brigadier, or sergeant, addressed himself to me, no doubt seeing that I had assumed a prominent place in the forefront, and seemed a person of importance.

'Monsieur here,' I said, pointing to the Colonel, who, in spite of all we could do, still held my lord tight, 'was the aggressor, as you can see for yourselves. Oblige him, I pray you, to desist. He will do my lord some serious injury.'

'Is one an English milord, *hein*? Who, then, is the other?'

'An abominable *vaurien*,' I answered with great heat. 'A rank villain; one who outrages all decency, breaks every law, respects no rank — '

'*Bus, bus*,' cried the Colonel, in some language of his own, as he put me aside so roughly that I still feel the pain in my shoulder. 'That'll do, my fine fellow. Let me speak for myself, if you please. Pardon, M. le brigadier,' he went on, saluting him politely. 'Here is my card. I am, as you will perceive, an officer of the English army, and I appeal to you as a comrade, for I see by your decorations, no doubt richly deserved, that you are an *ancien militaire*. I appeal to you for justice and protection.'

'Protection, forsooth!' I broke in, contemptuously. 'Such as the wolf and the tiger and the snake expect from their victim.'

It made me sick to hear him currying favour with the gendarme, and still worse that it was affecting the old trooper, who looked on all as *pekins*, mere civilians, far inferior to military men.

'Protection you shall have, *mon Colonel*, if you have a right to it, *bien entendu*,' said the sergeant, civilly but cautiously.

'I ask it because these people have made a dead set at me. They have tried to hustle me and, I fear, to rob me, and I have been obliged to act in my own defence.'

Before I could protest against this shameless misrepresentation of the fact, my lord interposed. He was now free, and, gradually recovering, was burning to avenge the insults put upon him.

'It is not true,' he shouted. 'It is an absolute lie. He knows it is not true; he is perfectly well aware who I am, Lord Blackadder; and that he has no sort of grievance against me nor any of my people. His attack upon me was altogether unprovoked and unjustifiable.'

'Let the authorities judge between us,' calmly said the Colonel. 'Take us before the station-master, or send for the Commissary from the town. I haven't the slightest objection.'

'Yes, yes, the *Commissaire de police*, the judge, the peace officer. Let us go before the highest authorities; nothing less than arrest, imprisonment, the heaviest penalties, will satisfy me,' went on my lord.

'With all my heart,' cried the Colonel. 'We'll refer it to any one you please. Lead on, *mon brave*, only you must take all or none. I insist upon that. It is my right; let us all go before the Commissary.'

'There is no Commissary here in Culoz. You must travel to Aix-les-Bains to find him. Fifteen miles from here.'

'Well, why not? I'm quite ready,' assented the Colonel, with an alacrity I did not understand. I began to think he had some game of his own.

'So am I ready,' cried his lordship. 'I desire most strongly to haul this hectoring bully before the law, and let his flagrant misconduct be dealt with in a most exemplary fashion.'

I caught a curious shadow flitting across my comrade Tiler's face at this speech. He evidently did not approve of my lord's attitude. Why?

I met his eye as soon as I could, and, in answer to my inquiring glance, he came over to me and whispered:

'Don't you see? He,' jerking his finger toward the Colonel, 'wants us to waste as much time as possible, while my lady slips through our fingers and gets farther and farther on her road.'

'Where is she?'

'Ah, where? No longer here, anyway.'

The train by which we had come from Geneva was not now in the station. It had gone on, quite unobserved by any of us during the fracas, and it flashed upon me at once that the incident had been planned for this very purpose of occupying our attention while she stole off.

'But, one moment, Ludovic, that train was going to Mâcon and Paris. My lady was travelling the other way — this way. You came with her yourself. Why should she run back again?'

'Ah! Why does a woman do anything, and particularly this one? Still there was a reason, a good one. She must have caught sight of my lord, and knew that she was caught.'

'That's plausible enough, but I don't understand it. She started for Italy; what turned her back when you followed her, and why did she come this way again?'

'She only came because I'd tracked her to Amberieu, and thought to give me the slip,' said Tiler.

'May be. But it don't seem to fit. Anyway, we've got to find her once more. It ought not to be difficult. She's not the sort to hide herself easily, with all her belongings, the nurse and the baby and all the rest. But hold on, my lord is speaking.'

'Find out, one of you,' he said briefly, 'when the next train goes to Aix. I mean to push this through to the bitter end. You will be careful, sergeant, to bring your prisoner along with you.'

'*Merci bien!* I do not want you or any one else to teach me my duty,' replied the gendarme, very stiffly. It was clear that his sympathies were all with the other side.

'A prisoner, am I?' cried the Colonel, gaily. 'Not much. But I shall make no difficulties. I am willing enough to go with you. When is it to be?'

'Nine fifty-one; due at Aix at 10.22,' Tiler reported, and we proceeded to pass the time, some twenty minutes, each in his own way. Lord Blackadder paced the platform with feverish footsteps, his rage and disappointment still burning fiercely within him. The Colonel invited the two gendarmes to the *buvette*, and l'Echelle followed him. I was a little doubtful of that slippery gentleman; although I had bought him, as I thought, the night before, I never felt sure of him. He had joined our party, had travelled with us, and seemed on our side in the recent scuffle, here he was putting himself at the beck and call of his own employer. My lord had paid him five hundred francs. Was the money thrown away, and his intention now to go back on his bargain?

Meanwhile Tiler and I thought it our pressing duty to utilize these few moments in seeking news of our lady and her party. Had she been seen? Oh, yes, many people, officials, and hangers-on about the station had seen her. Too much seen indeed, for the stories told were confusing and conflicting. One *facteur* assured us he had helped her into the train going Amberieu way, but I thought his description very vague, although Tiler swallowed the statement quite greedily. Another man told me quite a different story; he had seen her, and had not the slightest doubt of it, in the down train, that for Aix-les-Bains, the express via Chambery, Modane, and the Mont Cenis tunnel for Italy.

This was the true version, I felt sure. Italy had been her original destination, and naturally she would continue her journey that way.

Why, then, Tiler asked, had she gone to Amberieu, running back as she had done with him at her heels? To deceive him, of course, I retorted. Was it not clear that her real point was Italy? Why else had she returned to Culoz by the early train directly she thought she had eluded Tiler? The reasoning was correct, but Ludovic was always a desperately obstinate creature, jealous and conceited, tenacious of his opinions, and holding them far superior to those who were cleverer and more intelligent than himself.

Then we heard the whistle of the approaching train, and we all collected on the platform. L'Echelle, as he came from the direction of the *buvette*, was a little in the rear of the Colonel and the gendarmes. I caught a look on his face not easy to interpret. He was grinning all over it and pointing toward the Colonel with his finger, derisively. I was not inclined to trust him very greatly, but he evidently wished us to believe that he thought very little of the Colonel, and that we might count upon his support against him.

20

There were seven of us passengers, more than enough to fill one compartment, so we did not travel together. My lord very liberally provided first-class tickets for the whole of the party, but the Colonel took his own and paid for the gendarmes. He refused to travel in the same carriage with the noble Earl, saying openly and impudently that he preferred the society of honest old soldiers to such a crew as ours. L'Echelle, still sitting on the hedge, as I fancied, got in with the Colonel and his escort.

On reaching Aix-les-Bains, we found the omnibus that did the *service de la ville*, but the Colonel refused to enter it, and declared he would walk; he cared nothing for the degradation of appearing in the public streets as a prisoner marching between a couple of gendarmes. He gloried in it, he said; his desire was clearly to turn the whole thing into ridicule, and the passers-by laughed aloud at this well-dressed gentleman, as he strutted along with his hat cocked, one hand on his hip, the other placed familiarly on the sergeant's arm.

He met some friends, too, — one was a person rather like himself, with the same swaggering high-handed air, who accosted him as we were passing the corner of the square just by the Hôtel d'Aix.

'What ho! Basil my boy!' cried the stranger. 'In chokey? Took up by the police? What've you done? Robbed a church?'

'Come on with us and you'll soon know. No, really, come along, I may want you. I'm going before the beak and may want a witness as to character.'

'Right oh! There are some more of us here from the old shop — Jack Tyrrell, Bobus Smith — all Mars and Neptune men. They'll speak for a pal at a pinch. Where shall we come?'

'To the town hall, the *mairie*,' replied the Colonel, after a brief reference to his escort. 'I've got a particular appointment there with Monsieur le Commissaire, and the Right Honourable the Earl of Blackadder.'

'Oh! that noble sportsman? What's wrong with him? What's he been doing to you or you to him?'

'I punched his head, that's all.'

'No doubt he deserved it; anyhow, Charlie Forrester will be pleased. By-by, you'll see me again, and all the chaps I can pick up at the Cercle and the hotels near.'

Then our procession passed on, the Colonel and gendarmes leading, Tiler and I with l'Echelle close behind.

We found my lord awaiting us. He had driven on ahead in a *fiacre* and was standing alone at the entrance to the police office, which is situated on the ground floor of the Hôtel de Ville, a pretty old-fashioned building of grey stone just facing the Etablissement Thermale, the home of the far-famed baths from which *Aix-les-Bains* takes its name.

'In here?' asked my lord; and with a brief wave of his hand he would have passed in first, but the officers of the law put him rather rudely aside and claimed precedence for their prisoner.

But when M. le Commissaire, who was there, seated at a table opposite his *greffier*, rose and bowed stiffly, inquiring our business, my lord pushed forward into the front and began very warmly, in passable French:

'I am an aggrieved person seeking justice on a wrong-doer. I — demand justice of you — '

'*Pardon, monsieur, je vous prie.* We must proceed in order, and first allow me to assure you that justice is always done in France. No one need claim it in the tone you have assumed.'

The Commissary was a solemn person, full

of the stiff formality exhibited by members of the French magistracy, the juniors especially. He was dressed in discreet black, his clean-shaven, imperturbable face showed over a stiff collar, and he wore the conventional white tie of the French official.

'Allow me to ask — ' he went on coldly.

'I will explain in a few words,' began my lord, replying hurriedly.

'Stay, monsieur, it is not from you that I seek explanation. It is the duty of the officers of the law now present, and prepared, I presume, to make their report. Proceed, sergeant.'

'But you must hear me, M. le Commissaire; I call upon and require you to do so. I have been shamefully ill-used by that man there.' He shook his finger at the Colonel. 'He has violently assaulted me. I am Lord Blackadder, an English peer. I am entitled to your best consideration.'

'Every individual, the poorest, meanest, is entitled to that in republican France. You shall have it, sir, but only as I see fit to accord it. I must first hear the story from my own people. Go on, sergeant.'

'I protest,' persisted my lord. 'You must attend to me — you shall listen to me. I shall complain to your superiors — I shall bring the matter before the British ambassador. Do you realize who and what I am?'

'You appear to be a gentleman with an uncontrollable temper, whose conduct is most improper. I must ask you to behave yourself, to respect the *convenances*, or I shall be compelled to show you the door.'

'I will not be put down in this way, I will speak; I — I — '

'Silence, monsieur. I call upon you, explicitly, to moderate your tone and pay proper deference to my authority.' With this the commissary pulled out a drawer, extracted a tricolour sash and slowly buckled it round his waist, then once more turned interrogatively to the sergeant:

'It is nothing very serious, M. le Commissaire,' said the treacherous gendarme. 'A simple brawl — a blow struck, possibly returned — a mere *rixe*.'

'Between gentlemen? *Fi donc!* Why the commonest *voyous*, the *rôdeurs* of the *barrière*, could not do worse. It is not our French way. Men of honour settle their disputes differently; they do not come to the *police correctionnelle*.'

'Pray do not think it is my desire,' broke in the Colonel, with his customary fierceness. 'I have offered Lord Blackadder satisfaction as a gentleman, and am ready to meet him when and how he pleases.'

'I cannot listen to you, sir. Duels are in contravention of the Code. But I recommend you to take your quarrels elsewhere, and not to waste my time.'

'This is quite unheard of,' cried my lord, now thoroughly aroused. 'You are shamefully neglecting your duty, M. le Commissaire, and it cannot be tolerated.'

'I am not responsible to you, sir, and will account for my action *à qui de droit*, to those who have the right to question me. The case is dismissed. Gendarmes, release your prisoner, and let everyone withdraw.'

We all trooped out into the square, where a number of persons had assembled, evidently the Colonel's friends, for they greeted him uproariously.

'The prisoner has left the court without a stain upon his character,' the Colonel shouted in answer to their noisy inquiries.

'But what was it? Why did they run you in?' they still asked.

'I refer you to this gentleman, Lord Blackadder. Perhaps some of you know him. At any rate you've heard of him. We had a difference of opinion, and I was compelled to administer chastisement.' A lot of impudent chaff followed.

'Oh! really, pray introduce me to his lordship,' said one. 'Does your lordship propose to make a long stay in Aix? Can we be of any use to you?' 'You mustn't mind Basil Annesley; he's always full of his games.' 'Hope he didn't hurt you. He didn't mean it really;' and I could see that the Earl could hardly contain himself in his rage.

Then, suddenly muttering something about 'bounders' and 'cads,' he forced his way through and hurried off, shouting his parting instructions to us to join him as soon as possible at the Hôtel Hautecombe on the hill.

We followed quickly, and were ushered at once into his private apartment. It was essential to confer and decide upon some plan of action; but when I asked him what he proposed to do next, he received my harmless request with a storm of invective and reproach.

'You miserable and incompetent fools! Don't expect me to tell you your business. Why do I pay you? Why indeed? Nothing you have done has been of the very slightest use; on the contrary, through your beastly mismanagement I have been dragged into this degrading position, held up to ridicule and contempt before all the world. And with it all, the whole thing has failed. I sent you out to recover my child, and what have you done? What has become of that abominable woman who stole it from under your very noses?

Blackguards! Bunglers! Idiots! Fat-headed asses!'

'Nay, my lord,' pleaded Tiler humbly, for I confess I was so much annoyed by this undeserved reprimand I could not bring myself to speak civilly. 'I think I can assure your lordship that matters will soon mend. The situation is not hopeless, believe me. You may rely on us to regain touch with the fugitives without delay. I have a clue, and with your lordship's permission will follow it at once.'

I saw clearly that he was set upon the absurd notion he had conceived that the lady had gone westward, and I felt it my duty to warn the Earl not to be misled by Tiler.

'There is nothing in his clue, my lord. It is pure assumption, without any good evidence to support it.'

'Let me hear this precious clue,' said his lordship. 'I will decide what it is worth.'

Then Tiler propounded his theory.

'It might be good enough,' I interjected, 'if I did not know the exact contrary. The lady with her party was seen going in exactly the opposite direction. I know it for a fact.'

'And I am equally positive of what I saw,' said Tiler.

His lordship looked from one to the other, plainly perplexed and with increasing anger.

'By the Lord Harry, it's pleasant to be served by a couple of such useless creatures who differ so entirely in their views that they cannot agree upon a common plan of action. How can I decide as to the best course if you give me no help?'

'Perhaps your lordship will allow me to make a suggestion?' I said gravely, and I flatter myself with some dignity, for I wished to show I was not pleased with the way he treated us.

'Whether the lady has gone north or south, east or west, may be uncertain; and although I am satisfied in my own mind as to the direction she took, I am willing to await further developments before embarking on any further chase. To my mind the best clue, the real, the only clue, lies here, in our very hands. If we have only a little patience, this Colonel Annesley will act as a sign-post.'

'You think that some communication will reach him from the fugitives?'

'Most decidedly I do. I firmly believe that the lady relies upon him greatly, and will in all probability call him to her, or if not that she will wish to let him know how she has got on.'

For the first time in this unpleasant interview his lordship looked at me approvingly. He quite changed his tone and dropped his aggressive manner.

'I believe you are entirely right, Falfani, and cordially agree with your suggestion,' he said with great heartiness. 'Let it be adopted at once. Take immediate steps, if you please, to set a close watch on this pestilent villain Annesley; keep him continually under your eye.'

'We've got to find him first,' objected Tiler gruffly and despondently.

'It ought not to be difficult, seeing that he was here half an hour ago, and we can hunt up l'Echelle, who will surely know, and who I have reason to hope is on our side.'

'Do it one way or another. I look to you for that, and let me know the result without loss of time. Then we will confer again and arrange further. Leave me now.'

I accepted my dismissal and moved towards the door, but Tiler hung behind, and I heard him say timidly:

'May I crave your lordship's pardon — and I trust you rely on my entire devotion to your lordship's service — but there is one thing I most earnestly desire to do.'

'Go on.'

'And that is to follow my own clue, at least for a time. It is the right one I firmly believe, and I am satisfied it would be wrong, criminal even to neglect it. Will you allow me to absent myself if only for a few days? That should suffice to settle the point. If I fail I will return with all speed. If, as I hope and believe, I strike the scent, assuredly you will not regret it.'

'There's something in what you say. At any rate that line ought to be looked up,' said his lordship. 'I am willing to wait a day or two until you return or report, or unless something more definite turns up in the other direction. I suppose he can be spared, Falfani?'

'He will be no manner of use here, it will be better to let him go; let him run after his red herring, he'll precious soon find out his mistake.'

'We shall see,' said Tiler, elated and cocksure, and I freely confess we did see that he was not quite the fool I thought him.

21

On leaving his lordship I descended to the grand entrance to the hotel with the intention of beating up the Colonel's quarters in Aix. Although the hotels were certain to be crowded at this, the height of the season, the town is not really large, the visitors' lists are well posted with new arrivals, and there are one or two public places where people always turn up at some time or other in the day. The *cercle* or *casino* and its *succursale* the Villa des Fleurs, with their many spacious rooms, reading-room, concert-room, baccarat-room, their restaurants, their beautiful gardens, are thronged at all hours of the day with the smart folk of all nationalities.

I stood on the top of the steps waiting for the private omnibus that plies between the hotel and the town below, when I heard my name called from behind, and turning, was confronted by Jules l'Echelle.

'Hullo!' I cried, eying him suspiciously. 'What brings you up here?'

'The Colonel, my master — for I have taken service with him, you must know — sent me here to inquire whether we could have rooms.'

'Why does he choose this hotel of all others?' I asked in a dissatisfied tone, although in my secret heart I was overjoyed.

'It's the best, isn't it? Haven't you come here?'

'My Lord Blackadder has, but that's another pair of shoes. There's some difference between him and a beggarly half-pay Colonel who will very likely have to black the boots to work out his bill. They know how to charge here.'

'The Colonel, I take it, can pay his way as well as most people. Anyhow, he's coming to stop here.'

'For any time?'

'Likely enough. He said something about going through the course, taking the baths, and among the rest asked me to find out the best doctor.'

'That'll mean a lengthened stay; three weeks at least.'

'Well, why shouldn't he? He's his own master.'

'Then he's finished with that foolish business about the lady; had enough of it, I suppose; burnt his fingers and done no earthly good.'

'How do I know? It's not my business; but I fancy I have fallen into a snug berth, a soft job, better than making beds in a sleeping-car

172

and being shaken to death in express trains.'

'Good wages, if it's a fair question?'

'Fifty francs a week, *pour tout potage.*'

I looked at him hard, revolving in my mind how best to approach him. L'Echelle was a Swiss, and with most of his sort it is only a question of price. How much would it take to buy him?

'Well, how have you fared? Have you succeeded in getting your rooms? Will your Colonel move up?'

'What would his lordship say? Wouldn't like it much, I expect. Shall I prevent it? It will be easy to say there are no rooms. I'll do just as you please.'

'You're very obliging.'

'I'm willing enough to oblige, as I've always told you — at a price.'

'Put a name to it; but don't forget you've had something on account. Last night I gave you five hundred francs.'

'Bah! I want a lot more than that, a thousand francs down and fifty francs a day so long as I serve you. Do you agree to my terms?'

'My lord won't. He looks both sides of his money, and pays no fancy prices for a pig in a poke.'

'Then I'll take my pigs to another market. Suppose I let the Colonel know what you've been at, trying to tamper with me. This hotel wouldn't be big enough to hold him and your patron together.'

'Well,' — I hesitated, not willing to appear too anxious, — 'let's say, just for argument's sake, that you got what you ask, or something near it. I'm not in a position to promise it, no, not the half of it. But we'll agree what you'd do for us in return?'

'Anything you chose to ask.'

'Would you come over to us, belong to us body and soul? Think first of my lord, put his interests before the Colonel's; tell us what the Colonel's doing, his game from day to day, read his letters, and tell us their contents; spy on his actions, watch him at every turn, his comings and his goings; the houses he calls at, the people he meets, every move he makes or has in view?'

'If I promise to do all that will you promise not to give me away? You'll keep your own counsel and protect me from the Colonel? If he got a whisper I was selling him I'd lose my place and he'd half kill me into the bargain.'

'Not a soul shall know but my lord and myself. I must consult him, or you won't get the money.'

'But there is that other chap, the one who joined us at Culoz, and who was with you at the Commissariat, a new face to me. One of your own party, wasn't he?'

'To be sure, Tiler; he's on the job, too, came out when I did from London. But he's gone, left us half an hour ago.'

'For good and all? Sacked, dropped out, or what?'

'Gone to follow up a game of his own. He thinks he knows better than any one else; believes the lady has harked back, and is following her to Amberieu, Mâcon, Paris, England perhaps. God knows where. It's a wild goose chase, of course; but my lord leans to it, and so it is to be tried.'

'You don't agree?'

'How can I when I'm satisfied he's wrong? She was seen in the express for Modane, making for the Mont Cenis tunnel. Of course that's the true direction. She was aiming for Italy from the first; the other sister, the divorced lady, is there; we've always known that. Go back to England! Bah! absolute rot. I'd stick to my opinion against fifty fools like Tiler.'

'It's a bargain, then; I can count upon the cash? How soon shall you know? I'd like to begin at once; there's something I would tell you here, and now, that would interest you very much. But money down is my rule.'

'Let me run up and ask his lordship. I won't keep you five minutes.'

My lord gave his consent a little grudgingly, but was presently persuaded that it was to his own advantage to have a spy in the heart of the enemy's camp. That was soon seen when l'Echelle had pocketed his notes and gave us the news in exchange.

'Now that I'm my lord's man I don't mind telling you that the Colonel does not mean to stay long in Aix, not one minute longer than till the call comes.'

'He expects a call?'

'Assuredly. He wants you to think he's a fixture here, but he means to cut and run after my lady whenever she sends to him. He'll be off then faster than that,' he snapped his fingers, 'and you won't find it easy to catch him.'

'That's good. You'll be well worth your money, I can see. Only be diligent, watch closely, and keep us fully informed. We shall trust very greatly to you.'

'Your trust shall not be misplaced. When I take an employer's pay I serve him faithfully and to the best of my power,' he said with an engaging frankness that won me completely.

Lord! Lord! what liars men are and what fools! I might have guessed how much reliance was to be placed upon a man who, to my certain knowledge, was serving two masters.

Why should he be more faithful to my lord than to the Colonel?

22

The rest of the first day at Aix passed without any important incident. I was a trifle surprised that the Colonel did not put in an appearance; but it was explained by l'Echelle, whom I met by appointment later in the day. I understood from him that the Colonel had decided to remain down in the town, where he had many friends, and where he was more in the thick of the fun. For Aix-les-Bains, as every one knows, is a lively little place in the season, and the heart and centre of it all is the Casino. The Colonel had established himself in a hotel almost next door, and ran up against me continually that afternoon and evening, as I wandered about now under the trees listening to the band, now at the baccarat table, where I occasionally staked a few *jetons* of the smaller values.

He never failed to meet my eye when it rested on him; he seemed to know intuitively when I watched him, and he always looked back and laughed. If any one was with him, as was generally the case — smart ladies and men of his own stamp, with all of whom he seemed on very familiar terms — he invariably drew their attention to me, and they, too, laughed aloud after a prolonged stare. It was a little embarrassing; he had so evidently disclosed my business, in scornful terms no doubt, and held me up to ridicule, describing in his own way and much to my discredit all that had happened between us. Once he had the effrontery to accost me as I stood facing the green board on which the telegrams are exposed.

'Where have we met?' he began, with a mocking laugh. 'I seem to know your face. Ah, of course, my old friend Falfani, the private detective who appeared in the Blackadder case. And I think I have come across you more recently.'

'I beg you will not address yourself to me. I don't know you, I don't wish to know you,' I replied, with all the dignity I could assume. 'I decline to hold any conversation with you,' and I moved away.

But several of his rowdy friends closed around me and held me there, compelled to listen to his gibes as he rattled on.

'How is his lordship? Well, I hope. None the worse for that little *contretemps* this morning. May I ask you to convey to him my deep regrets for what occurred, and my sincere wishes for his recovery? If there is anything I can do for his lordship, any information I can give him, he knows, I trust, that he can command me. Does he propose to make a lengthened stay here?'

'His lordship — ' I tried vainly to interrupt him.

'Let me urge him most strongly to go through the course. The warm baths are truly delightful and most efficacious in calming the temper and restoring the nerve-power. He should take the Aix treatment, he should indeed. I am doing so, tell him; it may encourage him.'

'Colonel, this is quite insufferable,' I cried, goaded almost to madness. 'I shall stand no more of it. Leave me in peace, I'll have no more truck with you.'

'And yet it would be wiser. I am the only person who can be of any use to you. You will have to come to me yet. Better make friends.'

'We can do without you, thank you,' I said stiffly. 'His lordship would not be beholden to you, I feel sure. He can choose his own agents.'

'And in his own sneaking, underhand way,' the Colonel answered quickly, and with such a meaning look that I was half-afraid he suspected that we were tampering with his man. 'But two can play at that game, as you may find some day.'

When I met l'Echelle that same evening as

arranged, at the Café Amadeo in the Place Carnot, I questioned him closely as to whether his master had any suspicion of him, but he answered me stoutly it was quite impossible.

'He knows I see you, that of course, but he firmly believes it is in his own service. He is just as anxious to know what you are doing as you are to observe him. By the way, have you heard anything of your other man?'

'Why should I tell you?'

'Oh, don't trouble; only if I could pass him on a bit of news either way it might lead him to show his hand. If Tiler is getting 'hot' — you know the old game — he might like to go after him. If Tiler is thrown out the Colonel will want to give help in the other direction.'

'That's sound sense, I admit. But all I can tell you is we had a telegram from him an hour or two ago which doesn't look as if he was doing much good. It was sent from Lyons, a roundabout way of getting to Paris from here, and now he's going south! Of all the born idiots!'

'Poor devil! That's how he's made. It's not everyone who's a born detective, friend Falfani. It's lucky my lord has you at his elbow.'

We parted excellent friends. The more I saw of l'Echelle the more I liked him. It was a pleasure to work with a man of such acute perceptions, and I told him so.

Nothing fresh occurred that night or the next day. I was never very far off my Colonel, and watched him continually but unobtrusively. I hope I know my business well enough for that.

I was rather struck by a change in his demeanour. It was very subtle, and not everyone might have noticed it. He wore an air of preoccupation that spoke to me of an uneasy mind. He was unhappy about something; some doubt, some secret dread oppressed him, and more than once I thought he wished to keep out of sight and avoid my searching interrogative eyes.

'You're right,' said l'Echelle. 'He's down on his luck, and he don't want you to see it. He's dying for news that don't seem in a hurry to come. Half a dozen times to-day he's asked me to inquire if there's a telegram for him, and he haunts the hall porter's box continually in the hope of getting one. Have you heard any more from Tiler?'

'Yes, another mad telegram, this time from Marseilles. Fancy that! It will be Constantinople next or Grand Cairo or Timbuctoo. The folly of it!'

'What does my lord say?'

'Plenty, and it's not pleasant to bear. He's

181

getting fairly wild, and cart ropes won't hold him. He wants to go racing after Tiler now, and if he does he'll give away the whole show. I hope to heaven your boss will show his hand soon.'

'It's not for me to make him, you must admit that. But cheer up, *copain*, things may mend.'

They did, as often happens when they seem to be at their worst.

I have always been an early riser, and was specially so at Aix, now when the heat was intense, and the pleasantest hours of the day were before the sun had risen high. I was putting the finishing touches to my toilette about 7 a.m. when I heard a knock at my door, and without waiting permission l'Echelle rushed in.

'Already dressed? What luck! There is not a moment to lose. Come along. I've a *fiacre* at the door below.'

He gave the *établissement* as the address, and we were soon tearing down the hill. As we drove along l'Echelle told me the news.

'It's come, that satanic telegram, and just what he wanted, I'm prepared to swear. He simply jumped for joy when he read it.'

'But what was the message? Go on, go on, out with it!' I shouted almost mad with excitement.

'I can't tell you that, for I haven't seen it yet.'

'Are you making a fool of me?'

'How could I see it? He put it straight into his pocket. But I mean to see it pretty soon, and so shall you.'

'You mean to abstract it somehow — pick his pocket, or what?'

'Simplest thing in the world. You see he's gone to have his bath, he likes to be early, and he's undergoing the douche at this very moment, which means naturally that he's taken off his clothes, and they are waiting in the dressing-room for me to take home. I shall have a good quarter of an hour and more to spare before they carry him back to the hotel in his blankets and get him to bed.'

'Ha!' I said, 'that's a brilliant idea. How do you mean to work it out?'

'Take the telegram out of his waistcoat pocket, read it, or bring it to you.'

'Bring it; that will be best,' I interrupted, feeling a tinge of suspicion.

'But I must put it straight back,' continued l'Echelle, 'for he is sure to ask for it directly he returns to the hotel.'

Within a few minutes he had gone in and out again, carrying now one of the black linen bags used by *valets de chambres* to carry their masters' clothes in. He winked at me as he passed, and we walked together to a shady, retired spot in the little square where the cab-stand is, and sat in the newspaper kiosk on a couple of straw-bottomed chairs of the Central *café*.

'Read that,' he said triumphantly, as he handed me the familiar scrap of blue paper.

'Have got safely so far with nurse and baby — entreat you to follow with all possible speed — dying to get on. — Claire, Hôtel Cavour, Milan.'

'Excellent!' I cried, slapping my thigh. 'This settles all doubts. So much for that fool Tiler. My lord will be very grateful to you,' and I handed him back the telegram, having first copied it word for word in my note-book.

'It means, I suppose,' suggested l'Echelle, 'that you will make for Milan, too?'

'No fear — by the first train. You'll be clever if you get the start of us, for I presume you will be moving.'

'I haven't the smallest doubt of that; we shall be quite a merry party. It will be quite like old times.'

23

Colonel Annesley again

I had no reason to complain of the course of events culminating in the affair at Culoz. I defended to myself the assault upon Lord Blackadder as in a measure provoked and justifiable under the circumstances, although I was really sorry for him and at the poor figure he cut before the police magistrate and gendarmes. But I could not forget the part he had played throughout, nor was I at all disposed to turn aside from my set purpose to help the ladies in their distress. Every man of proper feeling would be moved thereto, and I knew in my secret heart that very tender motives impelled me to the unstinting championship of Lady Claire.

I was still without definite news of what had happened between the two sisters while I was covering their movements at Culoz. I could not know for certain whether or not the exchange had actually been effected, and I did not dare inquire about the station, for it might betray facts and endanger results. I had no hope of a message from Lady Henriette, for she would hardly know where to address me. Lady Claire would almost certainly telegraph to me via London at the very earliest opportunity, and I was careful to wire from Culoz to the hall porter of my club, begging him to send on everything without a moment's delay.

Then, while still in the dark, I set myself like a prudent general to discover what the enemy was doing. He was here in Aix in the persons of Lord Blackadder and his two devoted henchmen, Falfani and Tiler. I had heard the appointment he had given them at the Hôtel Hautecombe, and I cast about me to consider how I might gain some inkling of their intentions. Luckily I had desired l'Echelle, the sleeping-car conductor, to stick to me on leaving the police office, and I put it to him whether or not he was willing to enter my service.

'I will take you on entirely,' I promised, 'if you choose to leave your present employment. You shall be my own man, my valet and personal attendant. It is likely that I may wander about the Continent for some time, and it may suit you to come with me.'

He seemed pleased at the idea, and we quickly agreed as to terms.

'Now, l'Echelle,' I went on, 'after last night I think I may trust you to do what I want, and

I promise you I won't forget it. Find out what the other side is at, and contrive somehow to become acquainted with Lord Blackadder's plans.'

'How far may I go?' he asked me plump. 'They are pretty sure to try and win me over, they've done so already. Shall I accept their bid? It would be the easiest way to know all you want.'

'It's devilish underhand,' I protested.

'You'll be paying them back in their own coin,' he returned. '*A corsaire fieffé corsaire et demi.* It will be to my advantage, and you won't lose.'

'Upon my soul, I don't quite like it.' I still hung back, but his arguments seemed so plausible that they overcame my scruples, and I was not sorry for it in the long run.

(The reader has already been told how Falfani craftily approached l'Echelle, and found him, as he thought, an easy prey. We know how the communication was kept up between the two camps, how Falfani was fooled into believing that he kept close watch over Colonel Annesley through l'Echelle, how the latter told his real master the true news of the progress made by Tiler. When there could be little doubt that the chase was growing warm and had gone as far as Lyons, the Colonel felt that there was danger and

that he must take more active steps to divert the pursuit and mislead the pursuers. The Colonel shall continue in his own words.)

I was much disturbed when I learnt that Tiler had wired from Lyons. I saw clearly what it meant. The next message would disclose the whereabouts of the Lady Claire, at that time the only lady, as they thought, in the case, and the lady with the real child. It would soon be impossible for me to make use of the second with the sham child to draw the pursuers after her. In this it must be understood that, although I had no certainty of it, I took it for granted that the little Lord Aspdale was with his aunt and not with his mother, who, as I sincerely believed, had already reached Fuentellato.

It was essential now to persuade my Lord Blackadder and his people that this was the case, and induce them to embark upon a hasty expedition into Italy.

I therefore concocted a cunning plan with l'Echelle for leading them astray. It was easy enough to arrange for the despatch of a telegram from Milan to me at Aix, a despatch to be handed in at the former place by a friend of l'Echelle's, but purporting to come from Lady Claire. My man had any number of acquaintances in the railway service, one or more passed daily through Aix with the express trains going east or west; and with the payment of a substantial douceur the trick was done.

The spurious message reached me in Aix early on the third morning, and the second act in the fraud was that l'Echelle should allow Falfani to see the telegram. He carried out the deception with consummate skill, pretending to pick my pocket of the telegram, which he then put under Falfani's eyes. The third act was to be my immediate exit from Aix. I made no secret of this, very much the reverse. Notice was given at the hotel bureau to prepare my bill, and insert my name on the list of departures by the afternoon express, the 1.41 p.m. for Modane and Italy. It was quite certain that I should not be allowed to go off alone.

And suddenly, like a bolt from the blue, came a complete change in the situation. Not long after I had consumed my morning *café au lait* and rolls, the conventional *petit déjeuner* of French custom, a letter was brought to my bedside, where, again according to rule, I was resting after my bath.

I expected no letters, no one except the porter of my London club knew my present address, and the interval was too short since my telegram to him to allow of letters reaching me in the ordinary course of the post.

I turned over the strange missive, the address in a lady's hand quite unknown to me, examining it closely, as one does when mystified, guessing vainly at a solution instead of settling it by instantly breaking the seal.

When at last I opened it my eye went first to the signature. To my utter amazement I read the name, 'Henriette Standish.' It was dated from the Hôtel de Modena, Aix-les-Bains, a small private hotel quite in the suburbs in the direction of the Grand Port, and it ran as follows:

Dear Colonel Annesley: — I have only just seen in the Gazette des Etrangers that you are staying in Aix. I also am here, having been unable to proceed on my journey as I intended after meeting my sister at Culoz. I thought of remaining here a few days longer, but I have also read Lord Blackadder's name in the list.

What is to be done? I am horribly frightened, and greatly vexed with myself for having put myself in this painful and most embarrassing position.

May I venture to ask your counsel and help? I beg and entreat you will come to me as soon as possible after receipt of this. Ask

190

for Mrs. Blair. Although I have never had the pleasure of meeting you, your extreme kindness to Claire emboldens me to make this appeal to you. I shall be at home all the morning. Indeed, I have hardly left the house yet, and certainly shall not do so now that I know he is here.

Always very gratefully and sincerely yours,

Henriette Standish.

Here was a pretty kettle of fish! Lady Blackadder in Aix! Was there ever such a broken reed of a woman? Already she had spoilt her sister's nice combinations by turning back from Amberieu when the road to safety with her darling child lay open to her. Now for the second time she was putting our plans in jeopardy. How could I hope to lure her pursuers away to a distance when she was here actually on the spot, and might be run into at any moment? For the present all my movements were in abeyance. I had reason to fear — how much reason I did not even then realize — they would be interfered with, and that a terrible collapse threatened us.

I dressed hurriedly and walked down to the Hôtel Modena, where I was instantly

191

received. 'Mrs. Blair' had given orders that I should be admitted the moment I appeared. I had had one glimpse of this tall, graceful creature, who so exactly reproduced the beautiful traits of her twin sister that she might indeed at a distance be taken for her double. There was the same proud carriage of her head, the same lithe figure, even her musical voice when she greeted me with shy cordiality might have been the voice of Lady Claire.

But the moment I looked into her face I saw a very distinct difference, not in outward feature, but in the inward character that is revealed by the eyes, the lines of the mouth, the shape of the lower jaw. In Lady Claire the first were steady and spoke of high courage, of firm, fixed purpose; the mouth, as perfectly curved as Cupid's bow, was resolute and determined, the well-shaped, rounded chin was held erect, and might easily become defiant, even aggressive.

Lady Henriette was evidently cast in another mould. Her eyes, of the same violet blue, were pretty, pleading, soft in expression, but often downcast and deprecating; the mouth and chin were weak and irresolute. It was the same lovely face as Lady Claire's, and to some might seem the sweeter, indicating the tender, clinging, yielding nature that commonly appeals to the stronger sex; but to me she lost in every respect by comparison with her more energetic, self-reliant sister.

I heard the explanation, such as it was, without the smallest surprise; it was very much what I expected now when I was permitted to know and appreciate her better.

'What shall I say, Colonel Annesley, and what will you think of me?' she began plaintively, almost piteously. 'But the moment I found I had to part with my child my courage broke down. I became incapable of doing anything. I seemed quite paralyzed. I am not brave, you know, like my dearest Claire, or strong-minded, and I quite collapsed.'

'But I hope and trust you have made the exchange. Lady Claire has little Lord Aspdale and has left you the dummy? Tell me, I beg.'

'Oh, yes, yes, we made the exchange,' she replied, in such a faltering, undecided voice that I doubted, and yet could not bring myself to believe that she was not telling the truth.

'So much depends upon it, you see. Everything indeed. It would be a very serious matter if — if — '

'The contrary was the case,' I wanted to say, yet how could I? I should be charging her directly with wilfully misleading me, and deceiving me in this moment of extreme peril.

'But what will happen now?' she said, her voice faltering, her eyes filling, and seemingly on the very verge of hysterics. 'What if Blackadder should find that I am here, and — and — '

'He can do nothing to you unless he has a right to act, unless,' I answered unhesitatingly and a little cruelly perhaps, regardless of the scared look in her face, 'you have good reason to dread his interference. Lady Henriette, you have not been quite straight with me, I fear. Where is little Lord Aspdale?'

'In there!' she pointed to an inner room, and burst into uncontrollable tears.

24

To say that I was aghast at the discovery of Lady Blackadder, or, as she preferred to call herself, Lady Henriette Standish, in Aix, and with the precious child, would but imperfectly express my feelings. For the moment I was so utterly taken aback that I could decide upon no new plan of action. I sat there helplessly staring at the poor creature, so full of grief and remorse that I was quite unable to rise to the occasion. I had counted so securely upon tricking Lord Blackadder into a barren pursuit that my disappointment was overwhelming and paralyzed my inventiveness.

Only by slow degrees did I evolve certain definite facts and conclusions. The most essential thing was to get Lord Blackadder away from Aix. So long as he remained he was an ever present danger; our game was up directly he awoke to the true state of affairs. He could appeal now to the police with better result than when claiming my condign punishment. How was he to be got away? By drawing him after me. Clearly I must go, and that not alone, but take them with me, following me under the positive impression that I was leading them straight to their goal. Not one hint, not the slightest suspicion must be permitted to reach them that their quarry was here, just under their feet. Undoubtedly I must adhere to my first plan. When I had gone on with the others at my heels, the coast would be clear for Lady Henriette, and she must double back once more and go into safe hiding somewhere, while the hunt overshot its quarry and rolled on.

So soon as Lady Blackadder recovered from her agitation, I essayed to win her approval of my plans. But the idea of parting from me now that she had laid hold of me was so repugnant to her that she yielded once more to her nerves.

'I beg and implore you, Colonel Annesley, not to leave me again. I cannot possibly stay here alone. Let me go with you, please, please. I'll do what you like, disguise myself, go third class, anything; but for goodness' sake don't desert me, or I don't know what will happen.'

'There is simply no help for it, Lady Henriette. You simply must. It is imperative that you should remain here at least for a day or two while the others clear out of your way. It would be quite fatal if they saw you or you came across them.'

'Oh, you're too cruel, it is perfectly inhuman. I shall tell Claire, I am sure she will take my part. Oh, why isn't she here, why did I let her leave me? I think I am the most wretched and ill-used woman alive.'

These lamentations and indirect reproaches rather hardened my heart. The woman was so unreasonable, so little mindful of what was being done for her, that I lost my patience, and said very stiffly:

'Lady Henriette, let us quite understand one another. Do you want to keep your child? I tell you candidly there is only one way to save it.'

'My darling Aspdale! Of course I want to keep him. How can you suggest such a horrid idea? It is not a bit what I expected from you. Claire told me — never mind what; but please understand that I will never give my baby up.'

I was nettled by her perverseness, and although I tried hard to school myself to patience, it was exceedingly difficult.

'Indeed, Lady Henriette, I have no desire to separate you from your child, nor would I counsel you under any circumstances to give it up. But quite certainly while you are here in Aix you are in imminent danger of losing it. You ought never to have kept it — it was madness to come here and run straight into the jaws of danger.'

'How was I to know?' she retorted, now quite angrily. 'I really think it is too bad of you to reproach me. You are most unkind.'

'Dear, dear,' I said fretfully, 'this is all beside the question. What is most urgent is to shield and save you now when the peril is most pressing.'

'And yet you propose to leave me to fight it out alone? Is that reasonable? Is it generous, chivalrous, to desert a poor woman in her extremity?'

'I protest, you must not put it like that. I have explained the necessity. Surely you must see that it would be madness, quite fatal for us, to be seen together, or for you to be seen at all. I must still hoodwink them by going off this afternoon.'

'And leave me without protection, with all I have at stake? If only Claire was here.'

'It wouldn't mend matters much, except that Lady Claire would side with me.'

'Oh, yes, you say that, you believe she thinks so much of you and your opinion that she would agree to anything you suggest.'

'Mine is the safest and the only course,' I replied, I am afraid with some heat. 'You must, you shall take it.'

'Upon my word, Colonel Annesley, you speak to me as if I were a private soldier. Be good enough to remember that I am not under your orders. I claim to decide for myself how I shall act.'

She was no longer piteous or beseeching; her tears had dried, a flush of colour had risen to her cheeks, and it was evident that her despair had given place to very distinct temper.

I was in a rage myself, and sprang to my feet with a sharp exclamation of disgust.

'Really, Lady Henriette, you will drive me to wash my hands of the whole business. But I came into it to oblige your sister, and I owe it to her to do my best without reference to you. I have marked out a line for myself, and I shall follow it. Unless you are disposed to change your views, I shall stick to mine; and I do not see the use of prolonging this interview. I will bid you good day.'

I moved towards the door, still keeping an eye on her, believing her to be quite set in her fatuous refusal to hear reason. She still held herself erect and defiant, and there seemed to be small hope of doing anything with her. Then suddenly I saw symptoms of giving way. Signals of distress were hung out in her quivering lip and the nervous twitching of her hands. All at once she broke down and cried passionately:

'No, no, no; you must not leave me — not

like that. I cannot bear it; I am too miserable, too agitated, too terrified. I have no one to lean on but you. What shall I do? What shall I do?' And she collapsed into a chair, weeping as if her heart would break.

The situation was awkward, embarrassing. At another time I might have been puzzled how to deal with it, but this was a moment of supreme emergency. A great crisis was imminent, the ruin of our scheme and the downfall of our hopes were certainly at hand if I gave way to her. Everything depended upon my action, and I knew that the only chance of safety lay in the execution of my design.

This being so, her tears made no great impression on me. I may be called a hard-hearted brute, but I really had no great sympathy with her in her lamentations. It was not an occasion for tears, I felt; and I must be firm and unwavering, whatever she might think of me. I counted, at any rate, and with some assurance, on the approval of Lady Claire if the details of this painful scene should ever come to her ears.

Nor could I wait till she chose to regain her composure. Time was too precious to be wasted in any attempts to win her back to common sense, and without waiting for permission I crossed the room, rang the bell, and begged the waiter to summon the lady's maid. She was a strongly built, matter-of-fact French woman, probably not easily disturbed; but she glanced apprehensively at her mistress, and turned a suspicious look on me.

'You had better see to your lady,' I said sharply. 'She has an attack of nerves. I've no doubt it will soon pass, but I'm afraid I have imparted some distressing news. Be good enough to tell her when she recovers that I shall come back in half an hour, when I trust she will be ready to accompany me.'

'What is this?' broke in Lady Henriette, suddenly interposing and evidently roused to deep interest in my words. 'Accompany you? Where, I should like to know?'

'Is that of much consequence? You have entreated me not to leave you. Well, we shall not part; I propose to take you away with me. Do you object? It was your own wish.'

'I retract that. I will not go with you; certainly not in the dark. You must tell me first where you think of going, what you mean to do. Is it likely that I should trust myself alone with an almost complete stranger — a man who has shown me so little consideration, who has been so unkind, so cruel, and who now wants to carry me off goodness knows where, because he is so *obstinately determined* that his is the right way to proceed.'

'Lady Henriette,' I said civilly but very coldly, and putting the drag on myself, for I confess she was trying me very hard, 'let there be no misunderstanding between us. Either you consent to my proposals absolutely and unhesitatingly, or I shall withdraw altogether from your service. I have felt that I had a duty to Lady Claire, and I have been honestly anxious to discharge it, but by your present attitude I feel myself absolved from that duty. I am not unwilling to accept responsibility, but only if I am allowed to act as I please.'

'Oh, how like a man! Of course you must have your own way, and every one else must give in to you,' she cried with aggravating emphasis, giving me no credit for trying to choose the wisest course.

'I know I'm right,' I urged, a little feebly perhaps, for I was nearly worn out by her prejudice and utterly illogical refusal to see how the land lay. But I quickly recovered myself, and said quite peremptorily, 'You shall have half an hour to make up your mind, not a minute more, Lady Henriette. You shall give me my answer when I return. I warn you that I shall bring a carriage in half an hour, and I strongly advise you to be ready to start with me. Have everything packed, please, and the bill paid. I will take no denial, remember that.'

25

I returned to my hotel vexed and irritated beyond measure by my passage at arms with Lady Henriette Standish, and hating the prospect of any further dealings with her. I very cordially echoed her repeated cry for Lady Claire. Matters would have been very different had her strong-minded sister been on the spot to use her influence and help us with her counsel. What a contrast between the two women! I was more and more drawn to the one, and more and more heartily despised the other.

With my mind full of the beautiful creature who had made me a willing captive to her charms, her gracious presence was recalled to me by a message from under her own hand. As I passed the threshold of my hotel, the hall porter gave me a telegram from Lady Claire. It had come via London, but the office of origin was Marseilles.

Reached so far, yesterday. One of them turned up this morning — have no fear — exchange not effected — shall remain here for the present — Hotel Terminus.
  Claire.

I read and re-read this passage with a delightful feeling that it brought me into touch with my love, and I may be permitted for seeing in it clear proof of her bright wit and intelligence. She told me just exactly all that it was essential to know: of the pursuit, of the absence of pressing danger, of the abortive attempt to exchange babies, and where she was to be found. Suppose that I had not met Lady Henriette, I was fully prepared for anything that might occur.

It was now barely 10 a.m., and the time intervening before the departure of the eastward bound express (three and a half hours) was none too much to carry out my intentions as to Lady Henriette.

I first of all ordered a covered landau to be harnessed as speedily as possible, and to be sent to await me in a side street near the Hôtel Modena; then I summoned l'Echelle and bade him make all ready for the journey. I also told him that I should be busily engaged that forenoon; but that as I might be obliged to run it very close for the train, he was to make all preparations, to take the tickets, and await me on the platform. I had debated anxiously with myself how far I should betray the presence of Lady Henriette in Aix to l'Echelle, and decided that, although I had no particular reason to doubt him, I felt that it would be more prudent to keep the fact to myself. For the same reason I kept him busily engaged in my bedroom packing, lest he should spy upon my movements. There was still the fear that Falfani might be on the watch, but I had been assured by l'Echelle that the Blackadder party were so satisfied by the news he gave them that they left the business of shadowing almost entirely to him.

I was pretty sure that I reached the Hôtel Modena unobserved. I came upon the carriage by the way, and as I passed briefly desired the driver to follow me to the Hôtel Modena. Arriving there, I sent up my name, and followed it, a little unceremoniously, to Lady Henriette's sitting-room.

She was there, dressed in hat and jacket, and so far disposed to comply with my wishes. Her maid, Victorine, was with her, the baby on her knee. Her baggage, happily light enough, was there, packed and all ready for a start.

But if I thought that Lady Henriette meant to yield without another skirmish I was sadly mistaken. I was in for much more than a skirmish; it was to be a battle royal.

'The carriage is at the door,' I said as pleasantly as possible. 'We have nearly an hour's drive before us, and I am delighted to think that you are ready and willing to go with me.'

'I am ready, as you see, but not willing,' she answered, bridling up with a scornful air. 'Very much the reverse indeed. The more I think over it the more outrageous and preposterous your behaviour seems. Where are we going? I insist upon knowing. I must have a plain categorical answer or I will not move an inch.' Her dogged, determined air was belied by her dress and the obvious preparations already made for departure. Her present attitude I set down to the vacillation of her character. She might make up her mind one moment and one way, and yet be quite prepared to change it the next.

'You are fully entitled to know where you are going, and I have not the smallest desire to keep it from you,' I replied, still speaking in a smooth, courteous voice. 'I propose that you should take up your residence for a time — the very shortest time possible — at Le Bourget, a small place at the head of the lake. You may know it; there is a snug little hotel in the village, the Dent du Chat. You will like it.'

'I shall not like it. I dislike the whole idea exceedingly. Why should I be buried alive in such an out-of-the-way spot?'

'It will be no worse than Fuentellato, a place you chose for yourself.'

'I have a house of my own there — my own servants. It is perfectly safe.'

'Not now, believe me, they will come upon you there; trace you easily and quickly, and they are capable of any violence to capture and deprive you of your treasure.' I pointed to the child on the maid's knee.

'I shall be more at their mercy here in Aix.'

'Be guided by me. I am certain of what I say. All will be well if you will only keep out of the way now for a few hours, perhaps at most a couple of days. If they do not find you at once they will never find you. Only let me have a short start ahead and I'll lead them a pretty dance, and take them further and further away. You may rely on it, and I assure you they will never be able to find you or do you any harm.'

'I wish I could believe you,' she said. 'If I could only believe in you and trust you as Claire does,' she murmured pathetically, still tortured by doubt. 'Why has Claire deserted me? If she were only here, or I knew where to find her!'

I was on the point of imparting my last news, but I checked myself. Lady Henriette had seen her last, and must be well aware of the direction she was taking to Lyons and Marseilles. It would only unsettle her to know that her sister was at Marseilles to-day, and would be at Genoa to-morrow. She would be mad to join her, and it was my most earnest wish that, for the present at least, Lady Henriette should keep quiet in the background with her charge.

'You will soon be able to communicate with her, no doubt. Of course you arranged that at Culoz?'

'We arranged nothing. It was all so hurried, and we had much to talk about. She was so hard on me when I declared I could not part with my blessed boy. We had words — '

'Ah!' I had heard enough to know that there had been a strong difference of opinion, a sharp quarrel probably, and that Lady Claire had not spared her sister at this fresh exhibition of ridiculous weakness.

'May I ask, please, whether you were to believe in me or not?' I resumed, taking up the discussion where I had left it. 'We must be moving if we are to go at all.'

Her acquiescence, now tardily given, was surly and ungracious.

'I suppose I cannot help myself; I am quite at your mercy. You may be sure I shall not easily forget this, or forgive your overbearing treatment. I will go, but under protest.'

She led the way herself and entered the carriage first, motioning to Victorine to hand her the baby and take her seat inside. She made no such sign to me, although I followed close behind. But I also got in without invitation, only explaining that it might not be wise to show myself on the box.

The coachman had his orders, and he drove off briskly along the Marlioz road till he reached the turning towards the head of the lake. In less than an hour we pulled up before the Hôtel Dent du Chat, a simple, unpretending hostelry, to which I had telegraphed in advance, stating my needs. We were received with profuse civility, the best of everything placed at our disposal, a best at which Lady Henriette, as I might have expected, turned up her nose, sniffing and scornful.

She uttered no complaint, she would not address a word to me; her air was one of lofty, contemptuous reserve; she intimated plainly that we were 'dead cuts.'

Only at the last, just as I was driving away and lifted my hat in farewell, she yielded to an impulse of despair, and seized my arm in almost frenzied appeal.

'You must not, you cannot desert me; I will not be left like this. No man, no gentleman would do it. I beg and implore you to remain within reach, somewhere near at any rate. I can never face this place alone.'

Her last appeal touched me to the quick. Once more I sought to explain the dire necessity for this act that seemed so barbarous, but she was deaf to all my arguments, and still clung to me nervously as I climbed into the carriage.

When at length I got away, and I persisted in leaving, being so fully satisfied it was for the best, her piteous, reproachful accents still rung in my ears, and I shall count that return drive to Aix as the most miserable hour I have passed in my life.

The whole episode had occupied much time, and it was already past one when I reentered the town. I drove straight to the railway station, and was met outside it by the faithful l'Echelle.

'Monsieur, monsieur, will you believe it? They have gone half an hour ago, and not by the eastern but the western express.'

'You saw them?'

'I spoke to them. Falfani himself told me of the change in their plans. The latest news from their man in the south was so positive, and has so convinced my lord, that he is hastening full speed to join Tiler, and they are only too delighted to leave you behind.'

I laughed aloud with intense satisfaction.

'You do not mind, monsieur? You have no reason to fear them?'

'Not the least in the world, they are playing into my hands. I, too, have changed my plans. I shall now remain in Aix for some time longer. I shall be glad to go on with the baths.'

But I was thinking really of that poor creature I had abandoned at Le Bourget, and overjoyed to think that I might now meet her wishes, and perchance regain something of her good-will.

Once more I took the road to Le Bourget, driving over by the first *fiacre* I could pick up on the stand, a much slower journey than the first, and it was nearly 3 p.m. when I reached the little hotel.

It was indeed a day of surprises, of strange emotions and moving incidents.

When I alighted and asked for 'Mrs. Blair,' I was answered abruptly that she was gone.

'Gone? When? How?' I cried, in utter amazement.

'Madame went very soon after monsieur,' said the *patronne*, in high dudgeon. 'She was not complimentary, she said this place was too *triste*, that it got on her nerves. She called me up and said I was to bring her the *Indicateur*. Then she must have a carriage as soon as it could be prepared to drive her to Culoz, fifteen miles away, meaning to take the train from there.'

'Not to Aix?'

'Assuredly not, for when I suggested that she could more easily find the train there she told me to hold my tongue, that she knew very well what she was about, and wanted no observations from me.'

To Culoz? She was bound then to follow her sister, I felt sure of it; and I was aghast, foreshadowing the new dangers opening before her.

26

The Lady Claire Standish has her say

It was as much as I could do to restrain myself when I saw my gallant knight, the Colonel, rush at that despicable creature, Lord Blackadder, and shake him. I wanted to put my head out of the window and cry, 'Well done!' But I saw the folly of it, much as I was delighted, and checked any demonstration of joy. I had no time to spare for anything outside our settled plan, so I jumped out on to the platform at once, and closely followed by Philpotts joined Henriette, and cried:

'Quick, quick, dear, the train goes on in less than ten minutes. Give me the child, we must exchange again.'

'What do you mean?' she gasped, and looked at me dazed and bewildered. 'Why should I part with my boy, my own boy! I cannot, indeed I cannot. Why? Why?'

'Because Blackadder is over there, and in another minute or two the child will be taken forcibly from you. Luckily I can still save it.'

'Oh, but please, Claire, please explain. I do not understand, not in the least. What am I to do? I haven't heard, I do not know.'

'Go on to Fuentellato with the dummy. It is the easiest thing in the world. They will follow you, Colonel Annesley will see to that, while I carry our darling to some secure hiding-place and keep out of sight until we can meet. There, do not, for heaven's sake, delay. Give me the child.'

'I can't, I can't. I will not part with it. My own, my precious babe. Never. Nothing will induce me.'

'Upon my word, Henriette, you are too aggravating and impossible. To think that now at the eleventh hour you should fail me and break down. Are you going to spoil everything! Let me take little Ralph;' and I put out my arms for the child, which Victorine held.

But the mother stood between us, seized the baby convulsively, and with a gesture of repulsion cried:

'Go away, go away, you shall not have him. I don't care what happens, I will keep him against all the world.'

I pleaded and stormed in turn, I tried everything but force, all without avail. My foolish sister seemed to have taken leave of her senses; she thought nothing of the nearly certain collapse of our schemes, her one overmastering idea was, like any tigress, to resist all attempts to deprive her of her cub.

Meanwhile the time ran on. Already the officials were crying '*En voiture*,' and I knew my train was timed to leave at five minutes past 8 a.m. If I lingered I should lose it, no great matter perhaps, seeing that the exchange, my principal object, had not been made; but if I remained with Henriette, she with her baby and I with mine, the whole of the artifice might at any moment be laid bare.

I had to decide then and there, and all I could think of at the time was to keep the enemy in the dark as to the doubled part of the baby. At first I thought of sending Philpotts on alone with her charge and remaining with Henriette. She was so helpless, so weak and vacillating that I had small hope of her getting through to Fuentellato by herself. That was clearly the wisest course, and I should have taken it, but I was sorely vexed and put out by her obstinate refusal to play her part; and I told her so.

'Once more and for the last time, Henriette, will you do what I want?' I asked her peremptorily.

She only hugged her baby the closer and whispered a soft lullaby.

'Then I shall go on with the other. It may be best. They may still be drawn after me, and leave you to your own devices. The only thing for you to do is to take the first train the other way, — it will be here in ten minutes, — keep low and you may get through into Italy unobserved.'

'Are you really deserting me?' she cried piteously. 'When shall I see you again?'

'I shall go round the long journey to Marseilles, by the South of France, and will join you at Fuentellato. There is no reason why you should not get there. Colonel Annesley will detain the others here, you may be sure of that. Good-bye, now,' and without another word Philpotts and I ran round, regained the up platform, resumed our seats by the narrowest margin and proceeded on our way to Amberieu.

The reaction from this agitating scene was little less than despair and collapse. So soon as I could bring myself to think calmly and at leisure, I realized that I had done a very foolish thing. Was it possible for Henriette to get off by herself? Hardly, she had not the nerve, I had almost said the wit, to escape alone from the toils and snares that encompassed her. I blamed myself, I became a prey to the bitterest self-reproach for having abandoned her, for allowing myself to give way to temper, and treat her so cruelly. As the train rattled on, one thought took possession of me. I must get out and go back instantly, at least at the very first opportunity. I must retrace my steps and return again to Culoz, where I hoped to be in time to support and strengthen her, please God save her from the consequences of my unkind and ill-considered action.

Accordingly, at the very next station, Virieu, I alighted. It was still no more than 8.21. In less than an hour I was in the return train and once more at Culoz, where, sending Philpotts to hide with her charge in the inmost recesses of the ladies' waiting-room, I vainly explored the station for any signs of Henriette, but to my delight she was nowhere in sight. I was fairly entitled to suppose that she had gone on.

The place was still in a turmoil, the consequences no doubt of the affray expressly begun by Colonel Annesley to befriend me. I narrowly escaped being seen by some of my enemies, but they were evidently too much preoccupied by their indignation at the outrage put upon that great personage, Lord Blackadder. I passed within an inch or two of my gallant Colonel and was sorely tempted to speak to him, but was deterred by the possible mischief it might entail.

I was relieved when they all took seats in the eastward bound train, going only as far as

Aix-les-Bains, where, as I heard it stated by the Culoz officials, the case was to be submitted to the Commissary of Police. I felt sure that my gallant Colonel would hold his own, I felt no very great concern for him. Although not fully satisfied as to Henriette, I was so far satisfied by coming upon all the parties, Ralph, Blackadder, and the rest, at Culoz, that she had disappeared from the scene without interference.

I had now to decide upon my own movements. I debated with myself whether I should not follow my sister to Fuentellato, to which I made sure she had gone, and I had every reason to hope that I could eventually join her there. But it seemed to be throwing away that same chance of mystification which I had always kept in view, which might have served me so well but for her weakness, and I still clung to my hope of drawing them after me on the wrong scent.

At one time I thought of venturing boldly into their midst and appearing openly at Aix; but this would probably end in abruptly pricking the bubble, and nothing more was to be done. I thought of sending Philpotts to hunt up the Colonel and convey a letter to him detailing my situation, and was much taken with this idea, which I presently rejected because I did not clearly see what good could come of it. I was tortured with doubts, unable to decide for the best, and at last, from sheer inability to choose, resolved to adhere to my original plan of travelling south.

I would at least go to Marseilles, which I could reach that very night, and once there would be guided by circumstances, seeking only to control them to the extent of reporting my whereabouts to Henriette at Fuentellato, and to the Colonel via London as arranged.

This as it proved was the very wisest course I could have adopted, as will presently appear.

I was doomed to a long wait at Culoz. There was no train due westward till 12.40, and I had to put in nearly three solid hours, which I spent in wandering into the village, where I found an unpretending *auberge* and a rather uneatable breakfast.

Everywhere I was met with wearisome delays. A slow train to Amberieu, a still slower cross journey to Lyons, which I did not reach till nearly 4 p.m., and learnt that another hour or more must elapse before the departure of the next Marseilles express.

The journey seemed interminable, but just as I was losing all patience, I received a fillip that awoke me to alertness, and set all my nerves tingling.

The man Tiler, the second detective, the man whom I had already befooled more than once, was there now on the platform, waiting like myself to embark upon the 5.19 train south to Marseilles.

He had come after me; that was perfectly clear. He, and he alone, and I rejoiced greatly that I had to do entirely with him. I had tried my strength with him more than once already, and felt myself his equal in guile. Although he owed me a grudge and would certainly be upon his guard, I thought myself strong enough to face and outwit him.

27

When I first caught sight of Mr. Ludovic Tiler he was busily engaged in conversation with one of the guards and a couple of porters. From his gestures, no doubt, he was describing our party, and I was half-inclined to walk up to him and say 'Behold!' But then I drew back hesitating. I did not fear him in the least, but he would be sure to draw the others to him, and I did not quite like the idea of having three of them on my hands at once, and with no Colonel on my side.

I could only communicate with Colonel Annesley by a roundabout process, and it might take him some time to reach me, even if he was not otherwise engaged by Henriette.

This Tiler man would of course stick to me and follow me if he had the faintest clue, and I let him have that by directing Philpotts to show herself, passing quite close to him and walking on towards the train. She was to return then to the waiting-room, where together we made some change in our appearance. There were other cloaks in the bundle of rugs, which we put on over those we were wearing. I got out a thick veil, and

Philpotts replaced her neat bonnet by a soft motor cap. More than all, we made away with the dummy child, broke up the parcel, resolved it into its component parts, a small pillow and many wraps, all of which we put away in the same convenient receptacle.

Tiler certainly did not recognize us as we walked separately to the train. He was looking for a party of two and a baby, and all he saw was one woman who might remind him of me, but without her attendant or any encumbrance. He had his suspicions, however, for as soon as we started he walked through the long line of *couloir* carriages, deliberately peering and prying, examining the passengers of every compartment. He passed us at first, and was much put out, I could see, disappointed no doubt, but he came back presently and stood for some time at our window, while I hid my face in among the rugs, and Philpotts cowered in a corner.

He came back more than once during the journey and stared. No doubt he would have taken a seat in our compartment, but it was reserved for *dames seules* or ladies alone. He was evidently in great doubt, so much so that I began to fear he would sheer off altogether. That we were the women he wanted was probably borne in on him, but what had become of the baby? I could enter into the workings of his mind on that point. What could we have done with it? Hidden it, left it somewhere on the road in the lost property office or at a foundling hospital? All sorts of suggestions probably presented themselves to him, but none would satisfy him; for why, he would reason, were we travelling to Marseilles or anywhere else without it?

To tie him still to our heels, I took the opportunity of having the compartment to ourselves to revive and reconstitute the dummy. The baby was quickly reborn behind the drawn blinds of the carriage, and when at last we arrived at Marseilles at 10.30 p.m. we sallied forth and marched in solemn procession to the Terminus Hotel under the very eyes of our watchful detective. I almost laughed in his face as we entered the lift near the outer door, and were carried up to our rooms upon the second floor.

I slept late, and when I woke, refreshed and fortified against anything that might come, I looked out on to the little square with its fringe of plane-trees, and saw my friend Mr. Tiler walking to and fro like a sentry on his beat. He had the hotel under observation that was clear, and it was little I should be able to do that day unknown to him.

It did not worry me in the least, for in the early hours of calm reflection that followed deep, restful sleep, I had thought out the course I should pursue. I no longer dreaded pursuit; let them all come, the more the merrier, and I meant to fully justify Mr. Tiler in calling them to him.

I dressed slowly, lingered leisurely over my *luncheon-déjeuner*, and then ordered a carriage, a comfortable landau and pair. I meant to lead my follower a fine dance, starting with the innocent intention of giving myself and my belongings an airing. It was a brilliant day, the Southern sun struck with semi-tropical fervour, the air was soft and sleepy in the oppressive heat. I brought out the baby undeterred, and installed it, slumbering peacefully, on Philpotts's knees in the seat before me, and lying back with ostentatious indifference, drove off in full view of the detective.

I shot one glance back as I turned down the long slope leading to the Grâce-à-Dieu Street, and was pleased to see that he had jumped into a *fiacre* and was coming on after me. He should have his fill of driving. I led him up and down and round and round, street after street, all along the great Cannebière and out towards the Reserve, where Roubion's Restaurant offers his celebrated fish stew, *bouillabaise*, to all comers.

Then when Mr. Tiler's weedy horse began

to show signs of distress, for my sturdy pair had outpaced him sorely, I relented and reëntered the town, meaning to make a long halt at the office of Messrs. Cook and Son, the universal friends of all travellers far and near. I had long had an idea in my mind that the most promising, if not the only effective method of ending our trouble would be to put the seas between us and the myrmidons of the Courts. I had always hoped to escape to some far-off country where the King's writ does not run, where we could settle down under genial skies, amid pleasant surroundings, at a distance from the worries and miseries of life.

Now, with the enemy close at hand, and the real treasure in my foolish sister's care, I could not expect to evade them, but I might surely beguile and lead them astray. This was the plan I had been revolving in my mind, and which took me to the tourist offices. The object I had in view was to get a list of steamers leaving the port of Marseilles within the next two or three days, and their destination. As everybody knows, there is a constant moving of shipping East, West, and South, and it ought not to be difficult to pick out something to suit me.

The obliging clerk at the counter gave me abundant, almost unending, information.

'To the East? Why, surely, there are several opportunities. The P. and O. has half a dozen steamers for the East, pointing first for Port Said and Suez Canal, and bound to India, Ceylon, China, and the Antipodes; the same line for Gibraltar and the West. The Messagéries Maritime, for all Mediterranean ports, the General Navigation of Italy for Genoa and Naples, the Transatlantique for various Algerian ports, Tunis, Bône, Philippeville, and Algiers, other companies serving the coast of Morocco and especially Tangier.'

Truly an embarrassing choice! I took a note of all that suited, and promised to return after I had made a round of the shipping offices, — another jaunt for Tiler, and a pretty plain indication of what was in my mind.

After full inquiry I decided in favour of Tripoli, and for several reasons. A steamer offered in a couple of days, Sunday, just when I wanted it, although it was by no means my intention to go to Tripoli myself. That it was somewhat out of the way, neither easy to reach nor to leave, as the steamers came and went rarely, served my purpose well. If I could only inveigle my tormentors into the trap, they might be caught there longer than they liked.

Accordingly, I secured a good cabin on board the S.S. *Oasis* of the Transatlantique, leaving Marseilles for Tripoli at 8 a.m. the following Sunday, and paid the necessary deposit on the passage ticket.

It was a satisfaction to me to see my 'shadow's' *fiacre* draw up at the door soon after I left, and Mr. Ludovic Tiler enter the office. I made no doubt he would contrive, very cleverly as he thought, to find out exactly what I had been doing with regard to the *Oasis*.

Later in the day, out of mere curiosity, I walked down to the offices to ask a trivial question about my baggage. It was easy to turn the talk to other matters connected with the voyage and my fellow passengers.

Several other cabins had been engaged, two of them in the name of Ludovic Tiler.

There was nothing left for me but to bide my time. I telegraphed that evening to Colonel Annesley, reporting myself, so to speak, and counted upon hearing his whereabouts in reply next day.

Tiler did not show up nor trouble me, nor did I concern myself about him. We were really waiting for each other, and we knew enough of each other's plans to bide in tranquil expectation of what we thought must certainly follow. When I was at dinner in the hotel restaurant he calmly came into the room, merely to pass his eye over me as it were, and I took it so much as a matter of course that I looked up, and felt half-inclined to give him a friendly nod. We were like duellists saluting each other before we crossed swords, each relying upon his own superior skill.

(We need not reproduce in detail the rest of the matters set forth by Lady Claire Standish while she and the detective watched each other at Marseilles. Tiler, on the Saturday morning, made it plain, from his arrogance and self-sufficient air as he walked through the hotel restaurant, that all was going well, and he had indeed heard from Falfani that he would arrive with Lord Blackadder that night.

Later on that Saturday a telegram from Culoz reached Lady Claire from Colonel Annesley giving the latest news, and bringing down Lady Henriette's movements to the time of her departure for Marseilles. He promised a later message from somewhere along the road with later information, and soon after 9 p.m. Lady Claire was told they were coming through by the night train, due at Marseilles at 4 a.m. next morning. Thus all the parties to this imbroglio were about to be concentrated in the same place, and it must depend upon the skill and determination of one clever woman to turn events her way.)

She goes on to say:

It was a shock to me to hear that Henriette still lingered on the fringe of danger, and I was very much disturbed at finding she might be running into the very teeth of it. But I trusted to my good fortune, and, better still, to good management, to keep her out of harm's way until the coast was clear.

I was on the platform at 10 p.m. watching for the Blackadder lot when they appeared. Tiler was there to receive them and spoke a few words to my lord, who instantly looked round, for me no doubt, and I slipped away. I did not wish to anticipate a crisis, and he was quite capable of making a scene, even at the hotel at that time of night. I was relieved at seeing him pass on, and the more so that he did not take the turn into the Terminus Hotel, my hotel, but went towards the entrance where a carriage was waiting for him. He meant of course to put up in the town, either at the Noailles or the Louvre.

I lay down to take a short rest, but was roused in time to be again on the platform at 4 a.m. to meet my friends. It was a joyful meeting, but we lost little time over it. Henriette was fairly worn out, and all but broke down when she saw me. The Colonel came to the rescue as usual, and said briefly, after we had shaken hands:

'Take charge of her, Lady Claire, I will see to everything now. We can talk later.'

'Can you be at the entrance to the hotel in a couple of hours' time? I shall want your advice, probably your assistance.'

'You know you have only to ask,' he answered, with the prompt, soldierlike obedience, and the honest, unflinching look in his eyes that I knew so well and loved in him. Here was, indeed, a brave, loyal soul, to be trusted in implicitly, and with my whole heart.

I felt now that I should succeed in the difficult task I had set myself. The plan I had conceived and hoped to work out was to send Lord Blackadder to sea, all the way to Tripoli, with Philpotts and the sham child.

28

We drove down, Philpotts and I, to the wharf where the steamers of the Transatlantique Company lie. The *Oasis* had her blue peter flying, and a long gangway stretched from her side to the shore, up and down which a crowd passed ceaselessly, passengers embarking, porters with luggage, and dock hands with freight. At the top of the slope was the chief steward and his men, in full dress, white shirts, white ties, and white gloves, who welcomed us, asking the number of our stateroom, and offering to relieve us of our light baggage.

One put out his arms to take the baby from Philpotts, but she shook her head vigorously, and I cried in French that it was too precious.

Next moment a voice I recognized said:

'Certainly they are there, and they have it with them. Why not seize it at once?'

'Not so fast, Lord Blackadder,' I interposed, turning on him fiercely. 'No violence, if you please, or you may make the acquaintance of another police commissary.'

I had heard the whole story of the affair at Aix from the Colonel, who I may say at once

I had seen shortly before, and who was at no great distance now.

'Go on, Philpotts, get down below and lock yourself in,' I said boldly. 'Our cabin is thirty-seven — ' checking myself abruptly as though I had been too outspoken.

'But, Lady Claire, permit me,' it was Lord Blackadder behind, speaking with quite insinuating softness. 'Do be more reasonable. Surely you perceive how this must end? Let me entreat you not to drive me to extremities. I mean to have the child, understand that; but we ought to be able to arrange this between us. Give it up to me of your own accord, you shall not regret it. Ask what you choose, anything — a pearl collar or a diamond bracelet — '

'Can you really be such a base hound, such an abject and contemptible creature, as to propose terms of that sort to me? How dare you think so ill of me? Let me pass; I cannot stay here, it would poison me to breathe the same air. Never speak to me again,' I almost shouted, filled with bitter shame and immeasurable scorn, and I turned and left him.

Down-stairs I found Philpotts in the cabin, busily engaged in putting her 'doll' to bed in the third berth.

'Are you at all afraid of being left with

these wretches?' I asked a little doubtfully, counting upon her devotion, but loth to lay too great a burden on her.

'Why, how can you suppose such a thing, my lady? What can they do to me? They will be furiously angry, of course, but the laugh will be against them. If the worst comes to the worst they will appeal to the captain, and they will get no satisfaction from him. I can take care of myself, never fear. You shall hear from Tripoli to the same hotel in Marseilles.'

'If we go on your letter will follow us. Come back there as soon as you possibly can and you will find further instructions. Now it must be good-bye, there goes the bell to warn people ashore. One last word: I advise you when well out to sea to go to my lord and offer to go over to his side and desert me altogether. Tell him you will help him to get the child, — that you will put it into his hands indeed, — at a price.'

'As if I would touch his dirty money, my lady!'

'It will be only spoiling the Egyptians! Squeeze all you can out of him, I say. But that is as you please. You know I shall always be your firm friend whatever you do, and that I shall never forget what I owe you.'

I should have said much more, but now the second bell was ringing, and if I was to carry out my scheme it was time for me to go.

On leaving the cabin I walked forward along the lower deck seeking another issue, the position of which I had fixed the day before, having visited the *Oasis* on purpose. In a minute I had emerged into the open air, and found myself in the midst of the sailors sending down cargo into the forehold. I should have been utterly confused, bewildered, and terrified, but I felt a strong, firm hand close on mine, and a quiet, steady voice in my ear.

'This way, Lady Claire, only a couple of steps,' said the Colonel as he led me to the side of the steamer farthest from the shore. A ladder was fixed here and a boat was made fast to the lowest rung. Carefully, tenderly guided by my ever trusty henchman I made the descent, took my seat in the stern of the small boat, it was cast loose, and we pushed off into the waterway. Half an hour later we were back at the Terminus Hotel.

For the first time in all that stirring and eventful week I breathed freely. At any rate the present peril was overpast, we had eluded pursuit, and had a clear time of perfect security to consider our situation and look ahead.

As soon as Henriette was visible, I went up to her room to talk matters over. She was very

234

humble and apologetic, and disarmed me if I had intended to take her to task for all the trouble and anxiety she had caused us. But when I magnanimously said, 'I am not going to scold you,' she was in my arms at once.

'Scold me! I should think not! I have been scolded quite enough these last twenty-four hours. I never met a man I disliked so much as your fine friend, that Colonel Annesley, the rudest, most presuming, overbearing wretch. He talked to me and ordered me about as if I was still in the schoolroom, he actually dared to find fault with my actions, and dictated to me what I should do next. I — I — '

'Did it, Henriette? Like a lamb, eh? That's a way he has, my dear,' I laughed.

'I don't envy you one bit, Claire. You'll be a miserable woman. You hate to give way, and he'll make you. He'll tame you, and lord it over you, he'll be a hard, a cruel master, for all he thinks so much of you now.'

'And does he?' What sweeter music in a woman's ear than to be told of the sway she exercises over the man of her choice?

'Why, of course, he thinks all the world of you. He would say nothing, decide nothing until you had been consulted. Your word is law to him, your name always on his lips. You know of your latest conquest, I suppose?'

'There are things one does not care to

discuss, my dear, even with one's sister,' I answered, rather coldly. I was a little hurt by her tone and manner, although what she told me gave me exquisite pleasure.

'Come, come,' Henriette rallied me. 'Make a clean breast of it. Confess that you are over head and ears in love with your Colonel. Why not? You are free to choose, I was not,' and her eyes filled with tears at the sad shipwreck of her married life.

I strove hard to calm her, to console her, pointing to her little Ralph, and promising her a future of happiness with her child.

'If I am allowed to keep him, yes. But how can I keep him after that wicked decision of the Court, and with such a persistent enemy as Ralph Blackadder? For the moment we are safe, but by and by he will come back, he will leave no stone unturned until he finds me, and I shall lose my darling for ever.'

The hopelessness of evading pursuit for any time sorely oppressed me, too. There seemed no safety but in keeping continually on the move, in running to and fro and changing our hiding place so soon as danger of discovery loomed near. We were like pariahs ostracized from our fellows, wandering Jews condemned to roam on and on, forbidden to pause or find peace anywhere.

Yet, after a pleasant *déjeuner*, the three of

us held a council of war.

'The thing is perfectly simple,' said my dear Colonel, in his peremptory, but to me reassuring fashion. 'I have thought it all out and can promise you immediate escape from all your difficulties. You must go as quickly as you can get there, to Tangier.'

'Tangier!' I cried, amazed.

'Yes, Lady Claire, Tangier. It is the only refuge left for criminals — forgive me, I mean no offence,' and he laughed heartily as he went on. 'You have broken the law, you are flying from the law, and you are amenable to it all the world over, save and except in Morocco alone. You must go to Tangier, there is no extradition, the King's warrant does not run there. You will be perfectly safe if you elect to stay there, safe for the rest of your days.'

'You seem very anxious to get rid of us and bury us at the back of beyond,' I said, nettled and unable to conceal my chagrin at the matter-of-fact way in which he wished to dispose of us.

'I venture to hope I may be permitted to accompany you, and remain with you — '

It was now Henriette's turn to laugh outright at this rather blunt proposal, and I regret to add that I blushed a rosy red.

'To remain with you and near you so long

as my services may be required,' he went on, gravely, by no means the interpretation my sister had put upon his remark; for he fixed his eyes on me with unmistakable meaning, and held them so fixedly that I could not look away. There could no longer be any doubt how 'it stood with us;' my heart went out to him then and there, and I nodded involuntarily, more in answer to his own thoughts than his suggestion. I knew from the gladness on his frank, handsome face that he understood and rejoiced.

'You see,' he went on, quickly, dealing with the pressing matter in hand, 'I know all about the place. I have soldiered at Gibraltar and often went over to Africa. It's not half bad, Tangier, decent hotels, villas furnished if you prefer it. Sport in the season, and plenty of galloping ground. The point is, how we should travel?'

I could be of service in this; my inquiries at Cook's had qualified me to act as a shipping clerk, and we soon settled to take a steamer of the Bibby Line due that afternoon, which would land us at Gibraltar in two or three days. Thence to Tangier was only like crossing a ferry. The Colonel's man, l'Echelle, was sent to secure cabins, and we caught the ship in due course. Three days later we were soon comfortably settled in the Hotel Atlas, just above the wide sweep of sands that encircle the bay. It was the season of fierce heat, but we faced the northern breezes full of invigorating ozone.

29

Tangier, the wildest, quaintest, most savage spot on the face of the globe, was to me the most enchanting. Our impressions take their colour from the passing mood; we like or loathe a place according to the temper in which we view it. I was so utterly and foolishly happy in this most Eastern city located in the West that I have loved it deeply ever since. After the trying and eventful episodes of the past week I had passed into a tranquil haven filled with perfect peace. The whole tenor of my life had changed, the feverish excitement was gone, no deep anxiety vexed or troubled me, all my cares were transferred to stronger shoulders than mine. I could calmly await the issue, content to enjoy the moment and forget the past like a bad dream.

It was sufficient to bask in the sunshine, revelling in the free air, rejoicing in the sweetness of my nascent love. We were much together, Basil and I; we walked together, exploring the recesses of the native town, and the ancient citadel, with its memories of British dominion; we lingered in the Soko or native market, crowded with wild creatures from the far interior; we rode together, for his first care was to secure horses, and scoured the country as far as the Marshan and Cape Spartel. I sometimes reproached myself with being so happy, while my darling Henriette still sorrowfully repined at her past, with little hope of better days. But even she brightened as the days ran on and brought no fresh disquiet, while her boy, sweet little Ralph, developed in health and strength.

A week passed thus, a week of unbroken quiet, flawless as the unchanging blue of a summer sky; not a cloud in sight, not a suspicion of coming disturbance and unrest. It could not go on like this for ever. To imagine it was to fall asleep in a fool's paradise, lulled into false serenity by the absence of portents so often shrouded and unseen until they break upon us.

One day a cablegram reached me from Philpotts. She had arrived at Marseilles on her return voyage from Tripoli, and was anxious that I should know without delay that we had not shaken off Lord Blackadder. They had recrossed the Mediterranean together in the same ship, the *Oasis*.

'So far all well,' she said, 'but am watched closely, will certainly follow me — send instructions — better not join you at present.'

This message fell on us two poor women like a bolt from the blue. Basil looked serious for a moment, but then laughed scornfully.

'His lordship can do us no harm. There is not the slightest fear. He may bluster and bully as much as he pleases, or rather, as far as he is permitted to go. We will place ourselves under the protection of the Moorish bashaw. I always intended that.'

'Not seriously?'

'Indeed, yes; I have already consulted our Minister. Sir Arthur is an old friend of mine, and he has advised me, privately, of course, and unofficially, to be on our guard. He can do nothing for us, but he will not act against us. If Lord Blackadder should turn up here, and sooner or later he will, most assuredly he will not assist him. He promises that. At the same time he can give you no protection. We must take care of ourselves.'

'You believe that Lord Blackadder will find his way to Tangier?'

'Most certainly. He has Philpotts under his hand, but he would not trust only to her. Diligent inquiry at Marseilles would be sure to reveal our departure for Gibraltar. He will follow with his men, they are well-trained detectives, and it will be mere child's play for them to track us to Tangier. You may look for them here any day. We must be ready for

242

them at all points.'

'There is no saying what Ralph Blackadder may not attempt.'

'Indeed, yes, he is equal to anything, guile of course, treachery, cunning, stratagem, absolute violence if the opportunity offers. It is of the utmost importance not to play into his hands, not to give him the smallest chance. The child must be watched continually in the house, awake and asleep, wherever he goes and whatever he does.'

'Then I think Henriette must be warned not to wander about the town and on the sands in the way she's been doing with Victorine and the child, all of them on donkey back. I don't think it's at all safe.'

But when I cautioned her she was not particularly pleased. Was she to have no fresh air, no change of scene? I grudged her the smallest pleasure, while I was racing up and down flirting and philandering with Basil Annesley all day and every day; she was to sit indoors, bored to extinction and suffering torments in the unbearable heat.

Basil and I agreed that it was cruel to restrict her movements even with such a good excuse, and had she been willing to accept the irksome conditions, which she certainly was not. We arranged a surveillance, therefore, unknown to her. The Colonel, his man, or myself invariably accompanied her or followed her within eyeshot; and we hired two or three stalwart Moors, who were always to be near enough to render help if required.

Then came confirmations of our worst fears. L'Echelle, who had been unaccountably absent one morning, returned about midday with news from the port. Lord Blackadder and his two henchmen had just landed from the *José Pielago*, the steamer that runs regularly between Cadiz and Algeçiras, Gibraltar, and Tangier. He had seen them in the custom-house, fighting their way through the crowd of ragged Jew porters, the Moorish egg merchants, and dealers in luscious fruit. They had mounted donkeys, the only means of conveyance in a town with no wheeled vehicles; and l'Echelle made us laugh at the sorry picture presented by the indignant peer, with his legs dangling down on each side of the red leather saddle. Their baggage was also piled on donkeys, and the whole procession, familiar enough in the narrow streets of Tangier, climbed the hill to the Soko, and made for the Shereef Hotel, reputed one of the best in Tangier, and lying outside the walls in the immediate neighbourhood of the British Legation.

L'Echelle, who seems an honest, loyal fellow, thought he would serve us best by marking them down, and, if possible, renewing his acquaintance with the detectives, one or both of whom he knew. After hanging about the outside of the hotel, he entered the garden boldly and went up to the shady trellised verandah where they were seated together, smoking and refreshing themselves after their journey.

L'Echelle was well received. Falfani, my friend of the Calais train, believed he had suborned him at Aix, and now hailed his appearance with much satisfaction. L'Echelle might again be most useful; at least, he could lead them to us, and he wisely decided to let Falfani know where we were to be found in Tangier. The fact would surely be discovered without him. It was better, he thought, to appear frank, and, by instilling confidence, learn all there was to know of their plans and movements.

My lord had gone to the Legation, Falfani told him at once, bombastically boasting that everything would yield before him. He had but to express his wishes, and there would be an end of the hunt. But my lord came back in a furious rage, and, regardless of l'Echelle's — a comparative stranger's — presence, burst forth into passionate complaint against the Minister. He would teach Sir Arthur to show proper respect to a peer of the realm; he would cable at once to the Foreign Office and insist on this second-rate diplomatist's recall. The upshot of it all was that his lordship's demand for help had been refused point-blank, and no doubt, after what the Colonel had heard, in rather abrupt, outspoken terms.

All this and more l'Echelle brought back to us at the Atlas Hotel. He told us at length of the outrageous language Lord Blackadder had used, of his horrible threats, how he would leave no stone unturned to recover his son and heir; how he would bribe the bashaw, buy the Moorish officials, a notoriously venal crew; how he would dog our footsteps everywhere, set traps for us, fall upon us unawares; and in the last extreme he would attack the hotel and forcibly carry off his property. As the fitting end of his violent declamation, Ralph Blackadder had left the hotel hurriedly, calling upon his creatures to follow him, bent, as it seemed, to perpetrate some mad act.

I confess I shuddered at the thought of this reckless, unprincipled man loose about Tangier, vowing vengeance, and resolved to go to any lengths to secure it. My dear Basil strove hard to console me with brave words inspired by his sturdy, self-reliant spirit.

But even he quailed at the sudden shock that fell upon us at the very same moment.

Where was Henriette?

After the first excitement, we desired to pass on the news brought by l'Echelle to her, and renew our entreaties for extreme caution in her comings and goings; and with much misgiving we learnt that she was not in the hotel. She had gone out with Victorine and Ralph as usual, but unattended by any of us. One Moor, Achmet El Mansur, was with her, we were told, but we did not trust him entirely. It had been l'Echelle's turn to accompany her, but he had been diverted from his duty by the pressing necessity of following Lord Blackadder. Basil and I had ridden out quite early on a long expedition, from which we only returned when l'Echelle did.

We dismissed our fears, hoping they were groundless, and looking to be quite reassured presently when she came back at the luncheon hour.

But one o'clock came, and two, and two-thirty, but not a sign of Henriette, nor a word in explanation of her absence.

Could she have fallen a victim to the machinations of Lord Blackadder? Was the boy captured and she detained while he was spirited away?

30

It was impossible to disassociate Lord Blackadder from Lady Henriette's mysterious disappearance, and yet we could hardly believe that he could have so quickly accomplished his purpose. We doubted the more when the man turned up in person at the Atlas Hotel and had the effrontery to ask for her.

Basil went out to him in the outer hall, and, as I listened from within, I immediately heard high words. It was like a spark applied to tinder; a fierce quarrel blazed up instantly between them.

'How dare you show yourself here?' began Basil Annesley.

'Who are you to prevent me? I come to demand the restoration of that which belongs to me. Take my message to those two ladies and say I will have my boy,' replied my lord.

'Do not try to impose on me, Lord Blackadder. It is the most impudent pretence; you know perfectly well he is not here.'

'I will not bandy words with you. Go in, you men, both of you, Tiler and Falfani, and seize the child. Force your way in, push that blackguard aside!' he roared in a perfect paroxysm of passion.

I could not possibly hold aloof, but called for help from the hotel people, and, with them at my back, rushed out to add my protest against this intemperate conduct.

A free fight had already begun. The three assailants, Ralph Blackadder behind egging them on, had thrown themselves upon Basil, who stood sturdily at bay with his back to the wall, daring them to come on, and prepared to strike out at the first man who touched him.

'At him! Give it him! Throw him out!' cried Ralph passionately. But even as he spoke his voice weakened, he halted abruptly; his hands went up into the air, his body swayed to and fro, his strength left him completely, and he fell to the ground in sudden and complete collapse. When they picked him up, there was froth mixed with blood upon his lips, he breathed once or twice heavily, stertorously, and then with one long-drawn gasp died in the arms of his two men.

It was an apoplectic seizure, the doctors told us later, brought on by excessive nervous irritation of the brain.

Here was a sudden and unexpected *dénouement*, a terribly dramatic end to our troubles if we could but clear up the horrible uncertainty remaining.

What had become of my sister and little Ralph?

While the servants of the hotel attended to the stricken man, Basil Annesley plied the detectives with eager questions. He urged them to tell all they knew; it should be made worth their while; they no longer owed allegiance to their late employer. He entreated them to withhold nothing. Where and how had Lord Blackadder met Henriette? What had he done with her? Where was she now?

We could get nothing out of these men; they refused to answer our questions from sheer mulish obstinacy, as we thought at first, but we saw at length that they did not understand us. What were we driving at? They assured us they had seen no lady, nor had the unfortunate peer accosted any one, or interfered with any one on his way between the two hotels. He had come straight from the Villa Shereef to the Hotel Atlas, racing down at a run, pausing nowhere, addressing no one on the road.

If not Lord Blackadder, what then? What could have happened to Henriette? Tangier was a wild place enough, but who would interfere with an English woman in broad daylight accompanied by her servant, by an escort, her attendant Moorish guide? Full of anxiety, Basil called for a horse, and was about to ride off to institute a hue and cry, when my sister appeared in person upon the scene.

'Getting anxious about me?' she asked, with careless, almost childish gaiety. 'I am awfully late, but I have had such an extraordinary adventure. Why, how serious you look! Not on my account, surely?'

I took her aside, and in a few words told her of the terrible catastrophe that had just occurred, and for a time she was silent and seemed quite overcome.

'It's too shocking, of course, to happen in this awful way. But really, I cannot be very sorry except for one thing — that now he will never know.'

'Know what, Henriette? Have you taken leave of your senses?'

'Know that I have discovered the whole plot of which I was the victim. My dear, I have found Susan Bruel, and she has made a full confession. They were bribed to go away, and they have been here hiding in Tangier.'

'Go on, go on. Tell me, please, all about it.'

'You must know we went out, the three of us, on our donkeys, and the fancy seized me to explore some of the dark, narrow streets where the houses all but join overhead. I got quite frightened at last. I was nearly suffocated for want of air. I could not even see the sky, and at last desired Achmet to get me out into the open, anywhere. After one or two sharp turns, we emerged upon a sort of plateau or terrace high above the sea, and in full view of it.

'There was a small hotel in front of it, and above the door was the name of the proprietor, would you believe it, Domenico Bruel!

'It was the name of Susan's husband, and no doubt Susan was there. I could not quite make up my mind how I should act. I thought of sending Achmet back for you or the Colonel, but I could not bear parting with him. Then, while I was still hesitating, Susan herself came out and rushed across to where I was, with her hands outstretched and fairly beside herself, laughing and crying by turns.

'"Oh, my lady! It *is* you, then? What shall I say to you? How can I tell you?' she began, quite hysterically. 'We behaved most disgracefully, most wickedly, but indeed it was Domenico's doing. He insisted they offered us such a large sum, enough to make us rich for life, and so we consented to come away here. I have never had one happy moment since. Can you forgive me?'

'All this she poured forth, and much more of the same sort. I could see she was truly sorry, and that it had not been entirely her fault. Besides, I began to hope already that, how we had found her, we might get the case reopened, and that wicked order reversed. It will be put right now, now that Ralph can no longer oppose it.'

I bowed my head silently, thankful and deeply impressed with the strange turn taken by events and the sudden light let in upon the darkness that had surrounded us.

The rest of the adventures that began in the sleeping-car between Calais and Basle, and came abruptly to an end on the North African shore, may soon be told. Our first act was to return to England at the very earliest opportunity, and we embarked that evening on a Forwood steamer direct for London, which port we reached in less than five days.

Town was empty, and we did not linger there. Nothing could be done in the Courts, as it was the legal vacation, but Henriette's solicitors arranged to send out a commission to take the Bruels' evidence at Tangier, and to bring the matter before The President at the earliest opportunity.

As for ourselves, I persuaded Henriette to take a cottage at Marlow on the Upper Thames, where Colonel Annesley was a constant guest, and Charlie Forrester. We four passed many idle halcyon days on the quiet river, far from the noise of trains, and content to leave Bradshaw in the bottom of the travelling-bag, where it had been thrown at the end of our feverish wanderings.

Once again we had recourse to it, however, when we started on our honeymoon, Basil and I. Once more we found ourselves at Calais with Philpotts, but no encumbrances, bound on a second, a far happier, and much less eventful journey by the Engadine express.

We do hope that you have enjoyed reading this large print book.

Did you know that all of our titles are available for purchase?

We publish a wide range of high quality large print books including:
Romances, Mysteries, Classics
General Fiction
Non Fiction and Westerns

Special interest titles available in large print are:
The Little Oxford Dictionary
Music Book
Song Book
Hymn Book
Service Book

Also available from us courtesy of Oxford University Press:
Young Readers' Dictionary
(large print edition)
Young Readers' Thesaurus
(large print edition)

For further information or a free brochure, please contact us at:
Ulverscroft Large Print Books Ltd.,
The Green, Bradgate Road, Anstey,
Leicester, LE7 7FU, England.
Tel: (00 44) 0116 236 4325
Fax: (00 44) 0116 234 0205

Other titles published by Ulverscroft:

THE DUEL AND
COLONEL CHABERT

Joseph Conrad and Honoré de Balzac

When Lieutenant D'Hubert is sent to arrest Lieutenant Feraud for wounding a civilian in a duel, Feraud truculently insists on fighting the other officer — sparking a deadly feud between the two Hussars which will erupt in recurrent duels across many miles and many years . . . The japes of the law-clerks in the office of M. Derville are interrupted by the arrival of an old man in a tattered box-coat, seeking the attorney. He claims he is Chabert — the brave cavalry Colonel, beloved by Napoleon, who was presumed slain at Eylau. And he wants M. Derville to win back the money and honour stolen away from him . . .